# of The Rainbow

Dr Chander Notaney

Name of Book: The 8th Colour of The Rainbow
Author: Dr. Chander Notaney
Book Design: Kingsbury Printers
Cover Design: Micromint - Shirley Aggarwal
Edition: 2014
Price: £7
ISBN: 978-969-9282-28-7

Kingsbury Printers

Tel: 020 8205 3117
www.kingsburyprinters.co.uk

Book is available from:

Dr. Chander Notaney
email: cdnotaney@hotmail.com
Rifat Shamim
email: rifat.shamim@gmail.com

The inspiration behind my aspirations

Life

"Life is an opportunity, benefit from it.
Life is beauty, admire it.
Life is a dream, realize it.
Life is a challenge, meet it.
Life is a duty, complete it.
Life is a game, play it.
Life is a promise, fulfill it.
Life is a sorrow, overcome it.
Life is a song, sing it.
Life is a struggle, accept it.
Life is a tragedy, confront it.
Life is an adventure, dare it.
Life is luck, make it
Life is life, fight for it."

_ _ Mother Teresa

Contents

Foreword

This is my third book. It is different from my two previous books. It is not one single story. It is collection of eight stories, all unconnected. These are tales based on true incidents which I have heard of or witnessed and not utopian fiction. You might find some of the happenings in the book which you may have seen yourself or even experienced. As it is said everybody has a 'skeleton in his cupboard' hidden away somewhere.

Though the ideas and concepts are mine, I alone cannot take all credit for writing this book. The main proof reading is done by my brother-in-law Gresh Wadhwani who kept critiquing candidly my stories and language of the narrative till he was satisfied.

The second contributor to my book in proof reading and editing is my daughter-in-law Aarti whose input in this book has given it a professional touch.

Third contribution is by my son Arun in bringing Aarti from America to England.

Last but not the least, my thanks to my elder son Ashok for telephone training on writing with the computer keyboard.

Any errors and imperfections however are, despite all the assistance received, singularly mine.

Chander Notaney

Latif

It was a hot, sultry afternoon, when it all began. Or perhaps it was much earlier. Who knows? One can never be certain when the idea first started taking shape, a volition, a mind of its own. One can only surmise about the subtle moods and movements in a person's mind. But that was it. It was truly a hot afternoon and Tasneem was trying to rest in the darkened room. The blinds were drawn, filtering the light, and the three-bladed ceiling fan was whirling almost soundlessly. Round and round it went, trapped like a large flat-winged bird on a tether. Tasneem, felt tied. She turned, and twisted on the large bed which she shared with her husband Mustafa who was away in Lahore. He would be away for at least two days or more, but the large bed always felt empty even with him there. She was frightened to think that even after four or five years, they were so close together and yet so far apart from each other.

"A happy couple," people would remark. What little they knew! What little they knew!

Tasneem crossed her legs and uncrossed them. She was ever so restless. The fan kept on turning round and round untiringly. She could hear Latif working away in the kitchen, humming to himself. She often wondered what he was singing about under his breath. Once she had asked him. He was embarrassed, turning pink, the blood rushing into those pale cheeks, and to his delicate ears. He lowered his head and mumbled something. For the following few days he had stopped singing. Then it had started again. Now as Tasneem lay on her bed, she could hear the soft singing, more like a lament. In the background was the sound of tap running. Was he washing the tea cups? Or was he shelling the peas as he had been asked and was now rinsing them?

A shaft of sunlight, sharp as a dagger, pierced through the gap between the blinds and the window, filling the room with gold, with myriads of dancing moves. Tasneem could sense the uncomfortable heat outside the window. It was as if a sudden gust of wind had moved billows of feathery but rainless clouds, freeing the sun to shine with all its might, scorching everything in its wake below. In the quiet room the beam of the light edged slowly across the floor and along the opposite wall. It was like an unfurled turban, bright yellow in colour, and it hurt her eyes. She turned her head away from it.

"Latif," she called out, furrowing her brow.

The humming ceased. In the silence the fan continued cutting through the hot, muggy air. Tasneem squinted her eyes as she looked at the wall opposite; it seemed as if the sunlight was growing in intensity. Again she called out, louder this time and a little irritated. At the same time she raised herself on her elbows and turned her head towards the open door as if her eyes were chasing the words.

Latif shuffled in and stood, head down, framed in the doorway, all fifteen years of him, hardly a boy, scarcely a man although there was a faint handsome fringe of a moustache on his youthful face. He was good-looking, handsome like many Pathan boys. In time he would fill up, have broader shoulders, and with a few more inches, perhaps, grow as tall as Mustafa. But for now, as he stood there in that open doorway, he was neither a man nor a boy - an adolescent. He was uncomfortable as he shifted his weight from one foot to the other as he looked at Tasneem lying there on the bed.

"Jee memsahib," he said, arms dangling, eyes darting about uneasily.

"Adjust that blind. The sun is hurting my eyes," she said as she lowered herself onto her back again. He took off his sandals and moved towards the window.

Perhaps that is when it all had started - when she had seen his silhouetted figure against the filtered sunlight, when she had pressed her thighs together and had turned her body slightly on one side.

"What are you doing?" she blurted out, impatiently.

"I am closing the blind," Latif said, without turning his head, "so that the sun does not shine on the wall." Perhaps there was irritation in his voice. Or perhaps she imagined it. The shaft of light was reduced to a blade-thin shine, sharp and bright, like a sword. He stood there fidgeting, as if trying to block that thin line with his own bare hands.

"O K, well done," she said, "Good, off you go."

Latif turned, looked straight at the door and walked quietly towards it. He wanted to go back to the kitchen. His eyes were focused on his sandals lying there and he pictured his feet slipping into them and walking away, scurrying away, but his hurried thoughts were interrupted.

"Is there cold water in the fridge?" she inquired. She need not have asked because she knew there were at least two bottles of cold water in the fridge.

"Jee memsahib," Latif said nodding his head.

"Bring me a glass of cold water." Tasneem said.

Tasneem sat up again and stared at Latif's receding figure. She clasped her arms tightly around her arched knees. She knew it was not a glass of water that she wanted. There were other thoughts in her head, unspoken thoughts, that she had not wanted to acknowledge but that they were there, lurking, like unsavoury shadows in semi-dark corners. Mustafa would be away for two days, two nights. Mustafa was supposed to give comfort, she mused, but what comfort was there, when he was with her? Impotent old fool, she murmured under her breath. She was angry with herself, with her thoughts.

She heard the refrigerator door open and shut. She heard the water being poured into a tumbler. Again she lowered herself onto her back. She wondered if he was a virgin, whether men could be virgins. She shook her head as if dismissing the thought. Latif entered the room with the small tumbler gripped firmly in his hand.

"How many times have I told you to bring the glass on a saucer," she wanted to shout out. Instead she spoke in a tender, caring voice, "you forgot, you silly boy." A smile formed on her face, a forced chuckle escaping her lips.

Latif made a half a turn to go back to the kitchen, but she stopped him. "Never mind, bring it here."

She beckoned him with her raised arm. The loose sleeve fell back revealing the pale flesh and the flabby muscles almost up to the shoulder. And beneath the thin muslin dress, or kurta, was the outline of the darkened nipples of her large breasts. Her arms, feet, face and head were all uncovered and revealed begum sahib half sitting, half lying on the bed. Her hair, normally tied at the back, hung loosely over her shoulders.

Latif felt distinctly uncomfortable, nervous and hesitant, wondering whether it had been proper to enter the room. He had been told that he should knock before he stepped into their bedroom, but that was when the door was shut or partly shut. Now it was fully open and she had called him in. And he had walked in without thinking. And now again for the second time.

Mustafa sahib was on his way to Lahore. Latif had carried the bags to the car and locked them in the boot of the Mercedes. And then sahib had driven off and Latif had shut the large double gate, as he always did, once the car left. But he had forgotten to padlock it.

4

Perhaps it was awful forgetfulness on his part even though sahib had reminded him to do so just as he was driving off. Latif had left the small gate unlocked also. Somewhere in the back of his mind he thought that memsahib was sure to send him out on an errand: perhaps to buy a few freshly-baked loaves of bread or some fruit from the stalls. He would lock the gates later. It was too early. That is what he had thought. He also knew that Mustafa sahib would be away for few days.

Perhaps he should have walked out of the gate then, and not walked back into the house. Perhaps that is what he should have done. But why? There was no cause for concern. No reason at all. Possibly he could not have imagined what was going to happen next?

Now Latif stood with the tumbler in his shaking hand; Tasneem made little effort to take it from him. What should he do? He could hear his heart pounding, his stomach tightening, his legs trembling. He stared at the concentric circles forming on the surface of the water in the tumbler but he did not know the word for it. He could sense his outstretched hand shivering, shaking, as if it was cold and Tasneem making no effort to take the tumbler from him.

"Latif," she said, "what are you thinking?"

The voice was soft, gentle. Not like the abrupt commands that she had usually hurled at him over the past fifteen months, that was her tone since that one Friday at the beginning of the new year when Latif was brought straight from a village to work in Tasneem's house. The next door neighbour had heard through the grapevine that she and Mustafa were looking for a young boy to work for them. They had agreed on the terms and Latif quickly settled in.

Now he was uncomfortable, even a little frightened. The gentle tone had unsettled him.

Tasneem sat up and touched his hand as she took the tumbler.

Perhaps that was the fatal moment when the hands touched,

when the die was cast. Who knows? Tasneem half sat, half leant back on the pillows as she drank the water, taking small sips at a time, looking at the youth, trying to read his mind.

Latif waited silently, still trying to figure out what she was thinking when she had asked for the cold water. He had forgotten the saucer. Yes that was true, he had forgotten the saucer, but he was in a hurry to do her bidding, to get her the water from the fridge.

"Alright take it away," she said. Again, as she handed him the empty tumbler, their hands touched almost as if it was deliberate.

She wanted to grab him there and then, pull him towards her, onto her. But it did not happen. Thoughts remained unfulfilled, unsatisfied. As Latif reached the doorway, she spoke in that soft, almost strange, voice of hers.

"Latif, do you know what a massage is." It was not a question but a statement. "My back is very sore," there was a sigh, a hint of pain, a longing, a loneliness in her voice.

Latif stood transfixed, rigid as if he was part of the door. He had his back towards her. He dared not turn. Two more steps, two small steps, to reach the awkwardly placed slippers, and he would be out of that bedroom altogether.

"Never mind," Tasneem said, "we'll talk about it later. Go and finish your work." Then turning her head towards the window she closed her eyes.

All kinds of unconnected thoughts raced through Latif's mind as he hurried back to the relative safety of the kitchen. He had a lot of chores to finish; for one thing, there was the evening meal to be prepared, and then there were the plants to be watered and the terrace to be swept. He grabbed the plate of peas and started shelling them. All afternoon he kept himself occupied. Only once, much later, had Tasneem looked in briefly and then without saying anything, had gone to the lounge. He had heard her switching on the television and the voices of the characters from some programme.

That evening the dinner was served and had passed uneventfully. As usual he had set the table, brought the dishes and stood near the kitchen door while she ate. She commended his mince and peas curry. He was pleased but had kept his eyes glued to the floor. He was even more careful as he cleared the two dishes and the basket with the one remaining chapatti from the table. He had maintained his proper distance as he had been taught and never looked at her directly when speaking though he had noticed the continued softness in her voice, so subtle, so different. It placed him at a disadvantage.

It was even more disarming when she asked him, out of the blue, about when he was going to get married. He had reddened and had bit his lower lip. He was shaking and was afraid that he might drop the dish he had in his hand. He could hardly stop the serving spoon rattling against the side of the bowl.

"You have a girl in the village you like?" She had continued. He did not know which way to turn. She had pushed her chair back and was leaning against it but had carried on gently tapping the table with her fingers.

"No memsahib."

Latif had felt trapped, naked and helpless, as he stood there between the lady of the house and the kitchen door. He thought his problems were over when she indicated that she had finished her meal. But she made no attempt to leave while he waited for her to rise. She seemed in no hurry. He felt as if his feet were shackled to the floor. He wanted to escape from her presence.

Ever since that afternoon he had felt uneasiness which was only intensified by an overpowering but distinct aroma, a perfume that had a sweet and sour scent of cloves that surrounded her. It had filled her bedroom and appeared to follow her as she moved around the house.

All he wanted was to clear up and have his own supper, by himself in the safety of the kitchen. But he stood there transfixed, silently staring at the table.

Finally, Tasneem stood up and walked back to her bedroom. She did not shut the door; the light streamed out into the hallway. Latif was thankful that she had not pursued the subject of his marriage. He did not know how he was to respond. And he was glad that she had not mentioned anything about her bad back again. He started clearing the table. He wanted to hurry, to eat his meal, wash up and then disappear into his room at the far end of the corridor. He would be alone, isolated and lonely, but he felt much safer and secure there.

It was strange, sleeping by himself in a room of his own. He had never imagined possible, never imagined he would have his own room that would be almost as large as his family's house in the village. His house was clustered with the others on the side of a hill, not far from the towering shadows of the mountains. There they lived off the land - long, narrow terraces that they painstakingly tilled, cared for like some precious jewel, watered and weeded by hand, harvested by hand. That was how it was, for him and his family, and for all the others nearby.

And like many young boys, he too, had listened to the stories from those older than him, of the towns and bazaars, and he too had dreams of going far away from the village and finding work in some big town.

He also thought of coming back home from the strange big town, a little richer, a little better off, perhaps with a bicycle of his own, a sewing machine for his mother and sister or a shining new rifle for his father.

And later, after he had been working for some time, he thought he might even get his father a revolver, like the one Mustafa sahib had. Latif had once seen it lying on top of the chest of drawers, when he had gone into their bedroom to fetch sahib's glasses. Yes, perhaps he would have that, and he would also have a bicycle of his own and could cycle all day long. He would weave in and out around the houses even if the roads in the village were rutted and dusty. But he knew he would have to wait for the cycle, for the sewing machine and the rifle, and everything else. It takes time. It takes time!

For now though Latif was glad to have food in his stomach and a bed and a room of his own. Yes, the day of working was long and tedious, at times boring, but he was comfortable. There were bleak days when memsahib's mood was foul, and he could do nothing right, but he was learning. After all, town people have a different way of life, and he was getting better at his job. But sometimes he made mistakes. Like carrying a tumbler of water in hand and not on a saucer. Or placing the knives and forks the wrong way around the plate. Even sahib could be sharp but he knew that was to be expected. He was a servant, and he was working for them. He never really knew, if they were pleased with his work, but over the course of time they had less reason to shout at him, and they enjoyed the meals he cooked, the chapattis that he made. Of course, he was learning and improving all the time.

He knew that, and they knew that, but they rarely uttered a word of praise. He did not expect it to be any different. He knew his place. Sometimes he would forget something on purpose so that they would say something, even shout at him. Instead they both sat there eating in silence, ignoring him completely, uttering curt commands - "Bring that, take this away, move quickly, hurry up." But at least then they were talking to him.

He missed the banter and chatter and fights with his brothers and sisters, and the cousins at home. But Latif knew he could not have everything. One day it would be different.

It was strange that Mustafa sahib had gone off to Lahore alone this time. A few times they had gone away together and left him alone in the house. They had locked him in and told him to stay there, not to go out and not to let anybody in. Mostly it was just for one day at a time, but once it was for two days and another time for three whole days. He got used to long spells of silence, the long emptiness. But he had eaten his meals at the table, and drank green tea in the lounge, like how sahib did while looking through the magazines and books. He pretended that he was reading them like they did in English and Urdu. Though he did not know how to read and write, he could now recognise many of the words in both languages. And now from the tone of their voices he learnt to decipher the intended meanings of some of the English words that they used, especially when they were quarelling.

He would sit in his sahib's chair and pretend that he was the master of the house, and then he would shift on to her chair and mimic some of her ways, like holding the teaspoon in the air, or pointing at something with it. And he would smile to himself, and move back to sahib's chair, as if it was the proper place for him. He did not go into their bedroom. That was always locked and they took the key with them.

It was good to be sahib even if it was only for a day or two. One day perhaps he would even drive a car, a silver Mercedes, like sahib did. But now he was worried. He had cleaned the dining table and had his supper. He was busy finishing his dishes and then he would hurry to the safety of his room.

Just then he heard her voice. Not loud. But soft, pleading.

"Latif, Latif. Come here."

Now what, he thought. He could not pretend that he did not hear her.

"I am coming memsahib," he said, reluctantly.

Latif stood in the bedroom doorway. She was reclining on the bed, the fan whirring away, the bedside lamp shining on her face, on her hair, on her bosom.

"There is some green tea in the cupboard, is there not?" And without waiting for a reply she continued, "can you make me some?"

She smiled.

"Yes memsahib," he replied and turned around.

"Look," she said, "make a little more and you can have a cup also. Have you eaten?"

He nodded.

"Good, green tea helps the digestion. It is good for the stomach," she said as she touched her midriff.

"Yes memsahib," he said and walked back to the kitchen, confused.

Some ten minutes later he returned carrying a tray with the pot of tea, a matching set of cup and saucer, a bowl of sugar and a teaspoon. He looked around, anxious, wondering where to place the tray. The bedside cabinet was cluttered with jars and ornaments.

"Bring it here," she said, sliding to one side of the bed and patted the space between her body and the edge. "Here, here. You can put the tray here. And be careful. You don't want to scald me." She said in a loving voice, laughing.

Latif bent down and gently, but nervously, placed the tray on the bed. There was the whiff of the same perfume that he had noticed at the dinner table but perhaps it was a little bit stronger just as it is after she had had her bath.

"But you have brought only one cup. I told you green tea is good for the stomach," and she said while patting her stomach to emphasise the point.

Latif stood there, transfixed, afraid that the tray would slip off the bed, or the teapot would topple over if she moved even a little bit more, the green tea would spill all over the bed and run all over her.

"Go, go, get a cup for yourself," she said quickly. The matching cup and saucer rattled on the tray.

He turned and walked back. When he returned with a cup and saucer in his hand she was sitting up and holding the teapot in her hand. He could see that she had already poured out the tea in her cup.

"Come bring your cup here." She spoke slowly, softly. "Come, I am not going to eat you up. Sahib is not here. It's just the two of us. You, too, can have a cup of tea. Green tea is good for health." She told him again, "bring your cup here". "Why are you shaking?" With her free hand she steadied his arm as he bent down, and she poured out the tea into his cup.

Latif straightened up, nervously holding the cup and saucer.

"Sit down here, on the edge of my bed," she said, pointing. She moved her feet to make some space for him.

Latif felt as if the room had shrunk. The silence was as sharp as a silent dagger while the two of them sipped their tea. He knew it was not proper what he was doing, but what could he do! Memsahib had instructed him and there was no way he would disobey her, defy her. But sahib was not there and Latif felt it was wrong to drink tea with her in the bedroom.

"It is good, is it not?" she enquired in a quiet voice, disturbing his already muddled train of thoughts.

"Yes, memsahib," he said, raising his head. From the corner of his eye he could see the bedroom door. He was shaking all over, afraid that he would slip off the bed, afraid that the cup would fall from his hand. He was aware that her feet were just a few inches from his body. And what was he doing sitting in sahib's room and drinking tea with memsahib? Nothing made sense to him. It was all wrong. It just did not add up. Then he remembered that he had not padlocked the gate. He knew he had to do that before he retired for the night.

Latif made an effort to get up.

"Sit, sit" Tasneem said, her hand pressing on his thighs. "Sit and have some more tea." She was holding the pot in her other hand. In the thick silence he could hear the lid rattling. From the corner of his eye he could see that the tray was sliding precariously towards the edge of the bed. He moved his arm to grab the tray, and crossed over her arm which was still over his thighs.

"Put the tray on the floor," she said, quickly and firmly. She placed the teapot next to her cup. Latif bent down and placed both his cup, saucer and the tray on the floor. He then sat up, prepared to leave the bedroom.

"I've got to lock the gate," he said arching upwards.

"Oh, never mind the gate," Tasneem said impatiently. "Nobody is going to come now." With that she pulled him onto the bed.

It happened so quickly, her hand on his crotch, legs entwined, chest heavy with their heaving and the heavy breathing. They did not hear the front door opening or sahib calling. And then there was Mustafa standing in the doorway.

"He attacked me. He is trying to rape me," Tasneem screamed, pushing Latif off the bed, covering herself hurriedly with the crumpled sheet. Latif lay on the floor, his thin, pale legs curled up in a fetal position.

Without uttering a word Mustafa walked up to the chest of drawers, pulled the revolver out, released the safety catch and shot Latif three times at point blank range. Then, throwing the gun on the bed he said, quietly, but firmly, "He attacked you, and you shot him." Then he walked to the door and without turning said "I am going back to Lahore. I forgot some papers." He pulled the door slamming it shut with a bang behind him.

Morality which depends upon the helplessness of a man or woman has not much to recommend it.

A 'no' uttered from deepest conviction is better and greater than a 'yes' merely uttered to please, or what is worse to avoid trouble.

Mahatma Gandhi

The Underdog

P eter worked for a local building society. He was a diligent, honest and sincere worker, who enjoyed good health. His manager was very pleased with his work. In his twenty years of service he had never been absent without leave from work. He was a keen gardener. He loved looking after his garden. He took it as a part of his hobby and also to get fresh air so that he would keep himself fit without unnecessarily wasting money on gym subscriptions.

Mary, his wife, was a gynaecologist. She worked in a well known local hospital and also had a flourishing private practice. She was very popular in her social circle. Most ladies would even consult her during her lavish parties. Despite her very busy daily schedules she had a broad fun-loving outlook on life. She organised a lot of parties to raise funds for charity. This often resulted in return invitations for her to many parties. People close to her thought that she was made by God in his spare time. God had given her beauty, brains and a great talent for cooking exotic dishes. She was always the talk of the town and had decorated her house tastefully without the help of any interior designer. Her patients held her in such high esteem that they would wait for any length of time to see her on her return, when she was away on holidays. Some ladies were envious of her so many gifted talents.

Peter considered himself lucky, but was unhappy because Mary spent very little time with him. They always met each other only at the breakfast table. Their evenings together were very rare because Mary was either busy delivering babies in hospital or seeing her private patients late into the evenings. Her maternity practice took her away from home most of the time. Her loyalty to private patients was so unstinting that she would not flinch from visiting them in the middle of the night in an emergency and deliver the baby herself if need be. Her patients would willingly pay her any amount of professional fee to have a baby delivered by her, as she was known to have the golden touch.

Mary and Peter loved going away on holidays. While Peter was interested in wild life and seeing forests and enjoying the natural scenery, Mary was more fond of shopping. Once they visited California and stayed at Yosemite National Park. It is situated in the central eastern portion of California. Over 3.7 million people visit Yosemite each year. Most of the people spend their time in the seven square miles of Yosemite Valley. Designated a World Heritage site in 1984, Yosemite is internationally recognised for its spectacular granite cliffs, waterfalls, clear streams, giant Sequoia groves and biological diversity. Almost 95% of the park is designated wilderness. The downslope movement of the ice masses cut and sculpted the U-shaped valley that attracts so many visitors for its scenic views.

They stayed at a luxurious boutique hotel in the valley and received the best service they could desire. Spending money was not a problem for them. Mary had a flourishing current income. Peter enjoyed the natural scenes of wilderness and the fascinating views of Yosemite Park. He was however disappointed that Mary did not spend much time with him, like on any other holiday they had together. She used to be out shopping most of the day and would return tired to the hotel bedroom when Peter was already sound asleep in bed. The only time they used to have together was in the mornings at breakfast, just as in their own home.

The surroundings and the scenery inspired Peter to write. He had been writing short stories for his local magazine but now he decided to write a fiction book. He had never before attempted writing a full length book but had so much material stored in his head that he thought it could well culminate in a full book. He remembered many of the holidays he had taken with Mary and the wonderful places they had visited.

He remembered the Victoria Falls (the smoke that thunders) which is a waterfall located in southern Africa on the Zambezi River between the countries of Zambia and Zimbabwe. David Livingstone, the Scottish missionary gave it the name 'Victoria Falls' in honour of Queen Victoria. While it is neither the highest nor the widest waterfall in the world, it is claimed to be the largest. The falls are formed as the full width of river plummets in a single vertical drop into a transverse chasm 1708 meters wide, carved by its water along a fracture zone in the basal plateau. The spray from the falls typically rises to a height of over 400 meters and sometimes even twice as high, and is visible from up to 48 km away. At full moon, 'Moon-Bow' can be seen in the spray instead of usual daylight rainbow.

Victoria Falls is roughly twice the height of North America's Niagara Falls and well over twice the width of its Horseshoe Falls. In height and width Victoria Falls is rivalled only by South America's Iguazu Falls. Peter had always wondered why Niagara Falls are more famous than Victoria Falls or Iguazu Falls. Perhaps their marketing and public relations bring tourists flocking to Niagara Falls. Peter always remembered that Mary was never interested in seeing these wonders of nature. She always found time to go shopping anywhere on holidays and hardly cared to see such fascinating spots in the world. Peter, most of the time, went alone to see such delightful scenic places in the world.

Mary had seen Peter writing away, when she had returned from a shopping spree but never bothered to ask, what he was doing with so much writing. Peter continued writing. He recalled the early days of his life. Coming from a middle class family he was keen to study and receive good education. His parents were very supportive of him and helped him go to university. He managed to gain his bachelor's degree in economics on a student loan. He was fond of reading and had a penchant for writing right from his university days. He had a good teacher at the university, who mentored him on the art of storytelling and often critiqued his written work.

During his final year Peter fell in love with Mary who was a medical student at the same university. Mary also liked him and they started going out together. Peter finished his degree first, as his was only a 3 year course; Mary had a 5 year course, taking longer to finish her degree. They continued seeing each other. After Mary qualified as a doctor, they got married in Canterbury Cathedral and had the good fortune to be married by the archbishop himself. Mary's parents knew the archbishop closely and very well. He agreed to conduct the whole ceremony personally.

Canterbury Cathedral in Canterbury, Kent, is one of the oldest and the most famous Christian structures in England and forms part of a World Heritage Site. It is the cathedral of the Archbishop of Canterbury. A pivotal moment in the history of Canterbury Cathedral was the murder of Thomas Becket in the north-west transept in 1170 AD by knights of King Henry 2. History has it that the king had a lot of conflicts with the strong-willed Becket and is believed to have said in frustration, "Who will rid me of this turbulent priest?" The knights took him literally at his word and murdered Becket in his own cathedral.

Peter and Mary had a rehearsal a week before the wedding, and learnt the whole wedding procedure. On the actual wedding day Peter and Mary's friends acted as ushers and came 45 minutes before the ceremony. Peter along with his close friend John as his best man, arrived before the wedding ceremony. Guests from both sides came 15 minutes before the ceremony began. The organist played the prelude music while they were being seated.

Mary, as the bride, entered the church next on the right arm of her father, her face covered with a veil. The bridal procession comprised of the chief bridesmaid, bridesmaids and pages. All the guests stood up as Mary started walking down the aisle. The archbishop was there to welcome Peter and Mary. Peter stood on the right of Mary and John the best man stood to the right of Peter, slightly behind him.

The opening hymn was sung;

One more step along the world I go
One more step along the world I go
From the old things to the new
Keep me travelling along with you
And it's from the old travel to the new,
Keep me travelling along with you

The archbishop explained to the gathering the reason of the ceremony and asked if anybody had any objection to this marriage. The archbishop then obtained agreement from Peter and Mary to be married and turning towards Mary's parents asked who was giving away the bride. Mary's father stood up nodding in reply and went and sat in the first row on the bride's side. The marriage vows were taken first by Peter and then by Mary. The archbishop blessed the rings and Peter and Mary put them on each other's fingers. The archbishop pronounced Peter and Mary as man and wife. Mary now lifted her veil and kissed Peter. The archbishop then asked them to sign the marriage register along with witnesses and handed the marriage certificate to Peter.

After the ceremony Peter and Mary proceeded to the church door along with their parents where photographs were taken. All the guests then moved to the reception hall where canapés and cocktails were being served to be followed by dinner. Food was delicious and drinks flowed freely. The reception was arranged and paid for jointly by Peter and Mary's parents. All the guests enjoyed the ceremonial refreshments. The archbishop was an amiable person and numerous guests took photographs with him which would keep as treasured memory of the day. Peter and Mary also came over to the reception hall and mingled with the crowd. Family and friends took in turns to take photos with them. They also enjoyed the delicious food and drinks. Champagne bottles were uncorked and everybody enjoyed the bubbly.

After the wedding the newly-wed couple went away for their

honeymoon to Venice in Italy. Venice is a city in north east Italy sited on a group of 118 small islands separated by canals and linked by bridges. It is located in the marshy Venetian lagoon which stretches along the shoreline between the mouths of the Po and the Piave rivers. Venice is renowned for the beauty of its setting, its architecture and its artworks. The city in its entirety is listed as a World Heritage Site, along with its lagoon. However the main place of prominence in Venice is San Marco.

Peter and Mary stayed in the Hotel Marconi Venice. The hotel overlooked the Grand Canal and the famous Rialto Bridge. They thoroughly enjoyed the ride in a Vaporetto (water bus), which is the main form of transport in Venice because of its canals. The ride down the Grand Canal is superb: amazing architecture, soft seaside sunlight and a fascinating parade of Venetian watercraft. They walked around St Mark's Square where they saw an amazing display of glassworks. Venice is famous for ornate glass work, known as Venetian glass. Murano glass is the world renowned, colourful and skillfully made. Mary was fascinated and shopped aplenty. They had a gondola ride in the Venetion canal serenaded by the gondolier. The merriment and delight of their honeymoon week in Venice was writ large on their faces and they got to know each other more intimately.

Life had become very busy for Mary after marriage. She was stretched in the hospital performing her duties as house officer, senior house officer and reaching the registrar grade. She wanted to make her career as a gynaecologist. She started studying for the FRCS (Fellow of Royal College of Surgeons) degree. She had to stay in the hospital three nights a week for her emergency duties. Peter was fully supportive of her to achieve her FRCS degree. Little did he realise that she would become even busier after she achieved her degree.

Time passed by relentlessly and Mary duly gained her FRCS. Peter and Mary were both very happy. Mary was offered a senior registrar's post with good prospects of becoming a consultant. She worked very hard and performed various complicated gynaecological operations under the supervision of an experienced gynaecologist.

Soon she became competent and confident and was able to undertake the complicated operations independently. She was offered the consultant post in gynaecology and was absolutely delighted.

Mary soon became a popular gynaecology surgeon and most of the patients preferred to see her. Her appointments were always booked for weeks in advance. She also started consulting in a private hospital becoming deeply involved in her work and career. Whilst Peter was very pleased with her progress, personally he was not too happy now that they hardly saw each other. Because of her workload she would invariably return home late every night while Peter was usually fast asleep. The only time they used to meet was at the breakfast table. Peter used to make breakfast for Mary as well. Even at breakfast they hardly had much time to talk to each other because Mary would often leave early for her hospital duties.

It was one such morning when, Mary and Peter were having their breakfast, the postman delivered a registered packet, addressed to Peter. Peter opened the packet and found that it was from his publisher, with an advance copy of his book. Peter looked at it and passed it on to Mary to have a look and to read it. Mary cursorily flicked through the pages and handed it back to Peter saying that she could not read it just then but would do so later when she had some more time. Peter also told her that his publisher had invited both of them to a party that evening. Peter was very disappointed when she politely refused his invitation to the party because she had an important meeting that evening. Peter wondered if she could postpone the meeting and come with him to the party. Mary explained that she could not postpone the meeting at such short notice and suggested Peter went to the party on his own.

Peter went alone to attend the publisher's party. He was introduced to a lot of other writers. He was pleasantly surprised that he had been awarded the Booker's first prize by the Literary Guild. All the writers appeared very impressed with his work, and more so because it was his first book.

21

The Booker prize for Fiction is a literary prize awarded each year for the best original full length novel, written in English language by a citizen of the Commonwealth of Nations. The winner of the Man Booker Prize is generally assured of international renown and success; therefore, the prize is of great significance for book trade.

The prize was originally known as the Booker-McConnel Prize after the Booker-McConnel Company began sponsoring the event in 1968. It became commonly known as "Booker Prize". The foundation is an independent charity funded entirely by profits of Booker Prize Trading Ltd. The prize money was originally £21,000, and was gradually raised to £50,000 in 2002. It is one of the world's richest literary prizes.

The book was based on his own life with a very candid description of his romantic affair with a young lady. It had a tragic ending. The lady died at a young age and the author had the courage to describe the intimate details of their love affair, pleasant memories, beautiful evenings together, refreshing discussions, petty arguments and making up at night in each other's arms.

The tragic death of the young lady was the most poignant part of the story. The protagonist was crestfallen after the young lady's death. He had to cope with life alone which he found difficult to come to terms with. His mental anguish was unbearable and very painful. He was only just living by reminiscing about those pleasant memories of their time together otherwise he would have long gone into depression.

Peter was congratulated very warmly by everybody and was requested to attend the official prize-giving ceremony at London's Guildhall along with his wife, where he would have the opportunity to meet and rub shoulders with the literati and the other prize winners. Peter was thrilled and gave this good news to his wife at night. Mary was very happy for him and promised that she definitely would attend the ceremony due to be held in two weeks.

Mary had all her appointments rearranged for that day and

accompanied her husband to the awards ceremony. Peter was in a state of ecstasy and during the cocktails Mary was being congratulated on her husband's success. The presiding chairman of the judging panel described Peter's book as a work of art. Though it was fiction, it was larger than life and very close to everybody's heart. Peter showed a potential of becoming a great writer since his first had received such accolades and had gone on to win the coveted Booker's first prize. There was a thundering round of applause when Peter received his award from the chairman.

After the prize-giving ceremony Mary heard some maunderings in the background about Peter's book. Some considered the story to be too saucy. Others thought it was naughty but nice, while others commented that it was a work of a genius. It had been written with artistic flair with intimate details of the love affair described vividly. There was one comment however which shocked Mary. She overheard the person seated behind her whispering to his friend that he could not fathom how the wife was able to tolerate such graphic description of her husband's passionate affair with another woman.

Mary was very upset and resolved to read the book fully as soon as she reached home. Upon reaching home, she straightaway went on to search for the book. She could not find it but felt hesitant in asking Peter about it. She made a mental note that she would buy a copy from the bookstore next morning on her way to work.

The next morning Mary did not wait for breakfast. She rushed out, telling Peter that she was in a hurry as she had some shopping to do before work. Peter told her that he would not be home that evening for dinner as he had a television interview and would be dining at the studio. Mary asked about the time of the interview. Peter was very proud to tell her that it was on Panorama at 9 pm on BBC 1. Mary was deeply impressed as Panorama is a well researched and a prestigious programme.

Panorama is a BBC television current affairs documentary programme. First broadcast in 1953, it is the world's longest-running programme. It has been presented by well known BBC presenters including Richard Dimbleby, Robin Day, David Dimbleby and Jeremy Vine.

Mary hurried to the nearest book shop on the High Street and learnt that the book was a best seller and fully sold out, having sold 10,000 copies in the first 2 weeks. The newsagent was awaiting a further delivery of the book the following week and promised to reserve a copy for her. He went on to tell Mary that it was a most interesting book which was making waves in the literary circles. He himself had read it three times already and found it very romantic, refreshing but also tragic and moving. Mary was very frustrated and disappointed at not being able to lay her hands on a single copy of the book that day. She could not concentrate on her work and had to cancel all her appointments for the evening. She rummaged through her husband's desk drawers at home, and eventually found a copy of the 'The Underdog'.

She was so engrossed in the book that she forgot her evening meal. She kept reading, with cups of black coffee providing her the necessary stimulant. She read the whole book in three hours. She was very upset to read the true story of her husband's love affair and was deeply touched by the intimate descriptions of his amorous liaison. As soon as she finished the book she realized that she was starving. Mary decided to make a snack rather than a full meal so that she did not miss the TV interview. She sat in front of the television with bated breath. Her heart was pounding and she had developed palpitations. She watched the presenter introducing Peter and congratulating him on the success of his book -The Underdog.

Peter was very modest about his achievement. The presenter politely asked him about his previous written work and lavished enormous praises on him for his overnight and runaway success. He was quite insistent to know the identity of the beautiful girl, who was now dead and with whom the author had such romantic affair. Peter had a faint smile on his face but tactfully avoided divulgeing the identity of that girl. He said he did not wish to demean his relationship and nor did he want to disparage his pleasant memories of her. Mary listened to every word carefully in an effort not to miss out on the name. When Peter came home that night Mary was very quiet, apart from congratulating him on the successful interview.

Mary could not sleep well that night. She tossed and turned the whole night. She woke up early and cancelled her hospital appointments and even her private clinic appointments. At the breakfast table Mary explained that she had taken the day off to visit her elder sister Catherine, who she hadn't seen for some time. Peter was quite surprised at this sudden turn of the events as Mary was not the type to cancel her hospital and clinic appointments at such short notice and that too for such a mundane reason.

At lunch with her sister, Mary sobbed her heart out about Peter's love affair. Catherine was aware of what Mary was talking about, as she too had read the book, and seen the interview on television. Mary felt so hurt and betrayed that she could not bear living with Peter any more. She wanted to leave him because she felt that not only had he been unfaithful but on top of it he had the audacity to reveal it to the public at large. She could not bear this insult and would not forgive Peter for it.

Catherine tried to mollify Mary's angst. She reassured Mary that the affair was over as this lady was no more and there was no use crying over spilt milk. Catherine advised Mary not to be hasty but talk to Peter about the girl, discuss the implications with him and then decide about their future. Mary paid heed to Catherine's advice and decided there and then that come what may she would find the identity of that girl today. She went straight home after lunch. She had rarely been home that early before and felt rather odd about it. She decided to cook the best meal she had ever cooked, that evening.

She decorated the dining table with freshly picked flowers and arranged them so beautifully that the table looked exquisite. She took time to make herself up too and looked absolutely gorgeous. She sprayed jasmine air freshener throughout the house. Jasmine was

Peter's favourite fragrance. Now she eagerly awaited Peter's arrival.

Peter entered the house shortly afterwards and was pleasantly surprised to find Mary at home. He also felt the pleasant whiff of jasmine wafting over the hall. Mary smiled at him and gave him a lingering and passionate kiss. Mary looked lovely that night. She asked Peter about his day at work and poured him his favourite drink. She asked him to freshen up before dinner as she had prepared something special for him.

When Peter entered the dining area, he was very impressed with the beautifully set dining table laid with steaming hot delicious food. He had missed this pampering for such a long time. At the dining table he politely enquired about her meeting with Catherine. Mary said that they had enjoyed a good lunch and a chat together.

Peter praised her for the delicious meal and her extra effort to make him very relaxed. Peter also told her how ravishing she looked that night. Mary accepted the compliment and asked whether he would like some coffee. He helped Mary clear the table and then they sat down next to each other cosily on the sofa, with their coffee.

They started talking about the old times and how they used to snuggle together and prattle on like this. Peter told Mary if love is the music, romance is the dance, and what a whirling, dizzying dance it is. Peter compared Mary with a summer's day as she was lovelier and more temperate and she walked like a beauty in the cloudless night, waxing lyrically about her. He reminded her of those romantic days when they used to dance together.

Peter kept on reminiscing about the happier days when they had time for each other. He went on: "You have been so busy with your work and parties that you have forgotten how much we used to love each other. I only have memories of those halcyon days when we had little money but plenty of love and time for each other. We used to sit together after dinner holding hands listening to the romantic melodies of Jim Reeves. I have relished the most delicious meal tonight after so many years. You truly are an excellent cook. It has revived the old memories. You are the glow in my heart but it is difficult to express the darkness that now dwells in there."

Mary also became very emotional and said that she had the love within her heart for him but conceded that she had been so preoccupied with her career that it had not been expressed. She went on: "My love for you will never fade even though my mind aspires for higher things. We should trust in our love and it will never wane. The sudden thought that you are not there for me makes me feel lonely and isolated."

Mary then abruptly changed the subject and wanted to talk about his book, the award and the ovation he had received. She told him that she was proud of him but was upset that he had described his love affair in print and was also very disturbed that he had such an affair without her knowledge. She would like to know the identity of that girl and also discuss their future together.

Peter looked into her eyes and asked: "Do you really want to know the name of that girl ?"

Mary replied: "I certainly do."

Peter smiled and said: "It is you my darling, there never was nor there is anyone else in my life."

Mary sounded puzzled: "But I am still alive, you said in your book that the girl you loved has died."

Peter smiled again, "Of course you are alive but it is our LOVE that has died. It is just symbolic, if our love has died, then my soul, my beautiful girl has died with it".

Peter told Mary that he had always loved her, and had never ever cheated on her. He loved her with all his heart and worshipped the ground where she walked. He had always admired and felt proud of her qualities, talents, skills and other attributes. But it was she who had neglected the love they have for each other. For him it was their love that had perished.

Mary looked at him with admiration and love, her eyes brimming and spilling and she cried. She gazed into Peter's eyes and said that, yes she was able to see the love in his eyes. She agreed that she had neglected her home and especially Peter because of her busy work schedule. In chasing money and her career she had let their love die. Mary held Peter's hands in hers and placed them on her heart. She promised to change. She would cut down on her private practice and stop doing those extra sessions in hospital.

True to her word Mary started coming home early. She started preparing delicious meals for Peter before he arrived home every day. Peter began enjoying home comforts once again. The house was filled with the fragrance of fresh flowers. They went out together over weekends enjoying summer walks and trying out different cuisine. On holidays Mary began to go with Peter to see places of interest all over the world rather than just go shopping. Peter started writing a new book in his spare time with happiness filled in his heart.

'The dormant love was rekindled by 'The Underdog'

"Woman is the companion of man gifted with equal mental capacities.
She has the right to participate in the minutest details in the activities of 'man' And she has an equal right of freedom and liberty with him"

Mahatma Gandhi 1917

The Quest for life

It was a crisp wintery afternoon in January. Aryan was at the Cambridge University graduation ceremony for the conferment of his degree in medicine, which he had achieved with distinction. The ceremony was attended by many prominent figures of the city, most of whom were in the social circle of his father Suresh Agarwal, an entrepreneur and a business tycoon. Aryan was the only son in the family. When Aryan went up on the stage to receive his award from the Vice Chancellor, his father suddenly had a heart attack and collapsed in the hall. He was rushed to the hospital but did not survive. Aryan was devastated.

At the funeral the next day the elite of the business community from the city thronged to pay their last homage to Aryan's father. There was a long procession of friends and relatives in the crematorium for the last rites. Mr Agarwal's sudden death was a massive shock for Aryan. He was left all alone in the world inheriting a vast estate of huge wealth, swathes of land and a string of properties. His hands were shaking and his whole body trembling. Aamir a loyal and close friend as well as business partner of Aryan's father stood beside him. He came forward and taking Aryan by the hand escorted him to the hearse to act as pall-bearers. They carried the casket bearing Aryan's father's body into the crematorium hall where the Vedic verses were recited by the priest and eulogies read out by Aryan and Aamir. The crowd gradually started thinning down after offering condolences to the bereaved one.

Aamir and Aryan drove back home. Aryan found it very hard

to come to terms with the untimely death of his father. Aamir tried to console him by reminding him of the stark reality of life that no one lives forever. Death is as certain as it is unpredictable. Whilst Aryan took great comfort from Aamir's words of solace, he remained in a state of disbelief over the sudden death of his much adored father. He missed his father. When he went to bed, he could not sleep a wink.

Images of his departed father kept appearing in front of Aryan's eyes. He was so much overwhelmed by these images that he started talking to his father who he felt was holding his hand and consoling him. Memories of all the incidents in his past began flooding back in his mind, since the time he was a small boy and how his father looked after him alone after the death of his mother. He was barely six years old when his mother died.

Aryan was born with the proverbial silver spoon in his mouth. His father Suresh Agarwal was a business tycoon dealing in export and import. Aryan never knew what merchandise his father dealt in, but he surely had made a fortune.

Mr Agarwal's London house was worth more than 5 million. He had a fleet of luxury cars in his driveway with a full-time chauffeur. Suresh Agarwal was keen to give Aryan good education. He was a brilliant student and easily gained admission to Cambridge. His father wanted him to get a degree in business management, so that he could take over his business. But Aryan had different aspirations for his life. He showed little interest in his father's business. For him, business meant wheeling and dealing.

Aryan was more inclined towards treating and healing the people rather than having to deal with merchandise and materials. His father respected his wishes and happily backed him in his pursuit of medical career. Aryan joined the medical college in Cambridge.

Aryan's mother was a simple woman and a perfect housewife with traditional Indian values. She never had the need to go out to work because her husband was already a multimillionaire. Unfortunately she died when Aryan was a small child.

Aryan was very happy in the medical college. He was a happy-go-lucky person. He easily made a lot of friends, but still could not find the ideal one, who he could call his true friend. He came from an affluent family and his friends knew it. He could afford to spend lavishly, throw parties and enjoy high life. His father was happy to support Aryan's extravagant lifestyle.

Aryan's only true friend who he could trust and rely on was Aamir, his father's business partner. Aamir was only a few years older than Aryan. Mr Agarwal had taken him on as a young apprentice in his company ten years ago. With his hard work and indefatigable attitude to whatever task he undertook, Aamir proved to be an indispensable and an invaluable asset to the business.

Mr Agarwal, an astute businessman himself, was quick to recognise these attributes in Aamir and aptly rewarded him by making him a partner in the company some five years ago. Suresh Agarwal was much impressed by Aamir's unstinting loyalty and integrity and came to regard him as a friend and treated him like a family member. Aamir never let him down. Aryan too regarded Aamir like an elder brother and his confidant. He had no qualms in confiding and discussing all his personal matters with him.

Five years on, Aryan was in the final year of his MBBS degree. His father was very proud and happy, and promised to attend his graduation ceremony in spite of the tight schedule in his business.

That date of 2nd January in the millennium year has remained indelibly etched in Aryan's memory when celebrations and tragedy took place on the same day. The Cambridge graduation ceremony is usually a special event in his college. He had gained his MBBS degree with honours.

Aryan remembered in flashback, when dressed in his graduation robes as he knelt down to receive his degree from the Vice

Chancellor he heard his father's loud cry of anguish instead of cheers in the background. His father had suffered a massive heart attack and later died on the operating-table during coronary bypass surgery.

The memory of the tragic death of his father always haunted Aryan. He made a firm resolve to become a heart surgeon with an even loftier ambition to pioneer a better technique to save other people, who suffered similar major heart attacks.

Aryan became a forlorn and lonesome person. The only person who kept him going through this melancholic phase in his life was his friend Aamir Khan. His sanity was restored with the sole efforts of Aamir. He encouraged Aryan to work hard at his studies and achieve his cherished goal of becoming a heart surgeon.

Heart surgery has made giant strides in the last 15 years becoming routinely common these days. Popularly called coronary artery disease, it is treated by either angioplasty or coronary artery bypass graft surgery (CABG). Coronary heart disease is the narrowing or blockage of coronary arteries which supply the blood to the heart muscles. It is caused by atherosclerosis or hardening of arteries due to build-up of fatty deposits called plaques. This result in chest pain called angina.

Coronary angioplasty or PTCA is a technique used in treatment of unstable angina and coronary heart disease. It is aimed at improving the blood supply to heart muscle. A flexible catheter like a hollow tube is inserted usually through groin to reach the coronary artery and the fatty blockage is crushed by inflated balloon and a metal stent is usually inserted to keep artery open.

Coronary bypass surgery is done when blockage cannot be relieved by angioplasty. In this operation the surgeon uses the blood vessel from the leg or arm of the patient to bypass the narrowed section of coronary artery and grafts into the good section of coronary artery.

Aryan was fascinated by the subject and by the recent advances in development of novel surgery techniques. After clearing his FRCS, he worked in Harefield Hospital a famous heart surgery hospital under renowned heart surgeons. It took him ten long years, before he became a well known heart surgeon in his own right in London.

Aryan was the most eligible bachelor around. He was not short of money to splash around. He became very friendly with numerous female acquaintances but no girlfriend. He felt that girls were after his money, so he never became serious with any girl. Mandakini was one girl whose company he did enjoy, but nothing more than that. She was in college with him and lived in the same neighbourhood. They had known each other since their childhood days. Aryan used to call her Mandy.

Aamir would often suggest to Aryan to get married and settle down in life, but Aryan always laughed it off. He used to say that life is to be enjoyed and that he was too young to get married. He was however determined that he did not want to get married to a woman who was interested only in his money.

One day out of the blue Aryan informed Aamir that he did not want to play around anymore and wanted to settle down in life. He asked where he could find a decent girl who would love him for what he was as a person and not for his money. Aamir suggested that he might find such a girl in India, where they might not know about his wealth and riches. Aryan liked this suggestion and agreed to go to India. He called up and spoke to a distant uncle in India and sought his help in finding a suitable match.

Aryan came to Mumbai, the vibrant commercial capital of India. His uncle briefed him about Indian women and Indian culture. Generally the Indian girls are smart but a little shy initially but once they like somebody, they love truly and are very faithful.

Aryan's uncle organised a few parties where he could meet some girls he might like. At one such party he met a girl called Seema. He could not take his eyes off her. He was totally smitten with her and invited her for a drink. She politely declined. After the party, he mentioned to his uncle about Seema. His uncle knew her parents and promptly arranged a meeting with them.

Seema's parents were very simple people. They wanted assurances that their daughter would be happy and will be well treated in London. They were a bit apprehensive at first at the thought of Seema going so far away from them. But Aryan assured them, that she could visit them in India whenever she wished and likewise they could come and see their daughter in London whenever they desired.

It was left to Seema to make the final decision. Seema wanted to know about Aryan's past girlfriends in London. He admitted that he was lonely in London and had some flings in the past but never a serious relationship with any girl. He gave her his word of honour that he would not have any more affairs after his marriage. Seema seemed satisfied with his assurances but asserted that she would hold him to his promise and word of honour if he ever strayed.

After the wedding, Aryan suggested a honeymoon in Las Vegas. Seema agreed and they arrived in Las Vegas – the Mecca of gambling world. Seema was fascinated with the various shows and gambling casinos. She felt as though she was in another world. Aryan was very keen on gambling but Seema exercised her restraining control on him.

Las Vegas is the most populous city in the U.S. state of Naveda. The city bills itself as The Entertainment Capital of the world. Established in 1905, Las Vegas was incorporated as a city in 1911. The famous Las Vegas strip is over 4 miles of illuminated stretch that can be seen from outer space. Seema soon got tired of the place after one week and was anxious to get to London and see her new home. In keeping with Seema's wishes, Aryan cut short their honeymoon and they headed back to London.

Seema was ecstatic at seeing her new house in London. She could easily sense that it lacked a woman's touch. With her talent and smart ideas she soon transformed the house into a warm and welcoming home.

Aamir suggested a grand reception at their home to celebrate their marriage. Aryan readily agreed and entrusted Seema and Aamir with the task of arranging the party and to make it a successful event.

The party was organised on a grand scale. Aryan's various friends and colleagues were invited. There were music and dance shows which were Seema's suggestion to create a mini Las Vegas ambiance. Drinks were flowing freely and the party was in full swing, when suddenly Mandy arrived and made a beeline for Aryan ushering him to a quiet corner. She told Aryan that she was expecting his child. She demanded one million pounds or else she would tell his new wife.

Aryan was not at all sure that he had slept with Mandy. In fact as far as he could remember, though he had quite few affairs, he had never been serious with any girl. He could not remember ever sleeping with Mandy. She reminded him of the new year party when he had a little too much to drink and had slept with her in her flat. Aryan still was not convinced but Mandy was quite obdurate.

Aryan did not want Mandy to tell Seema anything about their affair and her accusation about the pregnancy and create a scene at his party. He agreed to give her a million pounds provided that she arranged for an abortion immediately and went away from his and Seema's lives. Mandy agreed and collected the million pound cheque and promised to have an abortion carried out and never to return in their lives.

Seema had noticed Mandy talking to Aryan. After the party was over she found Aryan in a very sad and pensive mood. She asked Aryan the reason and specifically about his conversation with Mandy. Aryan did not lie. He told her all about Mandy and her pregnancy. Despite his strong denial that he had not slept with Mandy, Seema could not be convinced as he had already handed the cheque to Mandy. Seema felt deeply hurt. Seema told him that she too was pregnant with their child and was about to break the good news to him after the party. But now the situation had changed and she wanted to go back to India adding that he would never see her again.

Aryan was perturbed and ruffled at this sudden turn of events and could not control his emotions. His eyes were tearful and he begged her forgiveness. He pleaded with her that it was his past mistake and that he would never repeat it. Seema was too hurt to see his predicament and had made up her mind to leave him. Neither of them slept that night.

In the morning Seema packed her bags and booked a flight to India. Aryan kept on pleading and fell on his knees, but Seema would not budge.

Aryan asked whether she would consider coming back to him on any conditions she imposed. Seema at last relented and agreed to come back to him after one year provided that he behaved with propriety. She wanted him to stay in London without any contact with her or any other woman. She wanted a cast-iron guarantee that he would not engage in any extra marital affairs behind her back.

Seema confided in Aamir, who she also had come to regard as her brother and related the whole story. She made him promise that he would look after Aryan and also keep an eye on him while she was away. She urged him to make sure that Aryan would keep his promise for a year; otherwise she would never come back.

Aryan wanted Seema to let him speak to her during the delivery of their child. But Seema firmly put her foot down. He would only see her and their child when exactly one year had elapsed. Aryan though not happy, agreed to all her conditions because he genuinely cared for her. Seema made Aamir promise that if Aryan were to transgress then he would immediately inform her.

Seema left for India and Aryan began the countdown of the 365 days. Time seemed to stand still and it felt like 365 years to Aryan. He felt miserable and down in the dumps. The condition imposed by Seema not to have any affairs was hard but not to contact her for the whole year he found was harder still and very agonizing for Aryan.

Quite often Aryan thought about calling up Seema to ask about her well-being and pregnancy, but had to use a lot of will power to restrain himself. He believed that if he contacted Seema, he might risk losing her forever.

He was tempted to go out with so many willing girls, but his conscience would not let him. Aamir kept a close eye on him. Aamir had become promise-bound to Seema. Aryan felt very isolated and frustrated. Aamir advised him to apply himself fully to his work. Aryan buried himself in his work. Though he found it very hard, he kept going with fond memories of Seema, and of the few months they had been together.

While over in India Seema found it hard going as well. She missed Aryan and her home in London. She consoled herself by thinking of Aryan with the hope that he would keep his promise and turn over a new leaf for the sake of her love.

After nine months Seema gave birth to a lovely little girl. She wanted to let Aryan know but her own imposed condition prevented her from doing so. She named their daughter Sameera (breath of fresh air). She was a beautiful little baby with blue eyes and an ever smiling face.

Seema soon found out that looking after Sameera was a hard task. Though she had all the support of her parents, she felt that it was a full time occupation bringing up a little child. She realised that both parents were important in looking after a baby. She now knew that caring for a little baby on her own was very hard. Yet she was grateful to have Sameera for company.

At the age of six weeks Sameera started smiling. This brought immense joy and happiness to Seema. She started missing Aryan even more and wished her separation from Aryan for one year ended soon.

Over in London Aryan was also counting the days. He was aware that Seema would have given birth to their child but was dismayed that he could not contact her. He only wished and hoped that all had gone well with the birth of their child.

He was not sure whether Seema would inform him of her return. He calculated that the one year deadline would finish next Saturday and that Seema should arrive on Sunday. He could hardly bear the separation any longer and decided that he would wait at the airport from early Sunday morning. He was expectantly watching all the flights from India. The whole morning had passed but there was no sign of Seema. He was getting very frustrated and felt dejected. At last his prayers were answered when at about 2.30 pm he caught sight of Seema along with their little baby amongst the incoming passengers. He found Seema looked radiant and more beautiful than before.

Aryan also saw his cute little daughter Sameera with her blue eyes and a sleepy face following the long flight from India. He was very thrilled to see them both and hugged them dearly. Tears of joy rolled down his cheeks. He could hardly believe that Seema had at last come back to him after a year-long separation.

Seema too was very delighted to see Aryan. She noticed that he had lost weight and asked Aamir why he had not looked after Aryan. Aamir told her that Aryan had kept to his word and buried himself in his work but had neglected his diet.

Seema told Aryan that she had now forgotten the past and that she still loved him. They both agreed that they would start afresh and live the life of happiness with mutual love and respect.

Years passed by, Aryan and Seema were blissfully happy. Sameera was the cynosure of their lives becoming a source of their delight and inspiration.

They watched and witnessed Sameera growing up and noted down her various milestones. They saw her sitting at six months, toddling about at the age of one year, and starting to talk at around eighteen months. They became busy in their lives, with Sameera providing their greatest joy and relaxation.

They saw Sameera going to nursery, primary school, secondary school and then college to become a fashion designer. They did not realise how their little girl had grown up and turned into a beautiful young lady.

Soon Sameera's 21st birthday had arrived and they planned to celebrate it on a grand scale. Aryan and Seema worked together to organise the best party their friends had ever seen. The whole house suddenly erupted in a hive of activity. It was ornately decorated, adorned with flowers and illuminated with lights. Music and dance was organised.

Aryan and Seema were welcoming the guests, when suddenly Sameera entered the house accompanied by a handsome young man. Aryan and Seema were surprised to see her with a boy. They did not realise that she had grown up enough to bring a boyfriend home. They still thought of Sameera as their little girl.

Sameera introduced Rahul to her parents. She had known him for over a year which did surprise them, but they were very impressed with Rahul's genteel and respectful demeanour.

The party seemed to take on a new lease of life with Sameera and Rahul's arrival. Rahul was a singer and music maestro by profession. He had the god given gift of a fine voice. That evening he entertained and delighted the whole gathering well into the night. Seema and Aryan were also very pleased and the party ended on a happy note for all.

Next morning Seema and Aryan asked Sameera about Rahul, and how serious their friendship was. She said that they both were very serious about each other and were in love. Seema and Aryan had both liked Rahul and wanted to meet him again. Rahul was invited to tea the next day and they all had a pleasant afternoon and talked about future plans of Sameera and Rahul. Rahul was a music composer and regularly provided music for stage plays in London. He was in love with Sameera and wanted to marry her. Seema and Aryan were quite happy to give their consent, but wished to meet Rahul's parents first. Rahul told them how his father had died in a car accident a few years ago and now had only his mother as lone parent, who was a school teacher. He said that they were welcome to meet his mother and discuss further their plans for marriage.

Seema and Aryan went to meet Rahul's mother, with great anticipation, the following weekend at Rahul's house in Kent. They rang the doorbell. Rahul opened the door and ushered them to the sitting room. He apologised that his mum had to go to hospital unexpectedly to see her closest friend who had suffered a sudden stroke. She was expected back any time now. While they were waiting in the lounge for her, Aryan caught glance of a picture of a woman on the wall. He got up to have a closer look and to his utmost surprise he saw Mandy's picture. He could not believe his eyes and asked Rahul who she was. When he came to know that it was Rahul's mother's image, he was stunned. Rahul's mother was none other than Mandy, the woman Aryan allegedly had an affair with, and to whom he had given money to have an abortion done because she claimed that he was the father of the child.

Their visit turned into a disaster for Aryan. Seema noticed that Aryan's face had suddenly gone pale. He suspected that Rahul was his own son which meant Sameera and Rahul were half-brother and sister. Marriage between siblings is incest and deemed an offence and not permissible in Law. No sensible father would tolerate this anyway. Aryan was disconcerted and grim-faced. Rahul too was confused seeing a sudden change in Aryan's expression. Aryan got up and excused himself out of the house. Seema explained to Rahul that her husband had not been keeping well of late and they will come again some other time to see his mother. She followed her husband to the car and kept questioning him about the disastrous conclusion of their visit but he was too lost in the labyrinth of his past with flashbacks of his affair with Mandy. Eventually he confessed to Seema that Rahul probably is his son from Mandy even though he is not convinced but could not be sure.

Aryan and Seema had a blazing row that night. Seema accused Aryan of wreaking havoc in Sameera's life. Aryan's dark past and philandering ways had finally destroyed his family. Aryan in his defence said that he had given a million pounds to Mandy to have her pregnancy terminated and he wanted to ask Mandy why she had not gone through with the abortion.

Seema told Aryan that it is too late now to ask Mandy. This marriage between Rahul and Sameera now cannot take place. When Sameera came to know about the fiasco of the meeting and disapproval of her father to her marriage with Rahul, she became disconsolate and distraught. Rahul was also upset and could not understand the negative attitude of Sameera's parents. Sameera was so shaken that she avoided talking to her parents and adopted an indifferent attitude towards them.

It was a late night of winter, Sameera was not back home. Seema and Aryan were getting extremely worried about her. They frantically tried to contact all her friends but could not trace her. Seema got hysterically furious with Aryan and put all the blame on him for the upheaval caused in their family. In the heat of their arguments Sameera and Rahul entered the house looking weary and irate. Aryan and Seema rushed towards Sameera and hugged her and asked where she had been and the reason for coming home so late. Sameera burst into tears. But Rahul very politely and calmly brought it to their notice that they had already decided to get married with or without their consent. Sameera told them that she had come to collect her essential stuff. She felt sorry that she had to leave the house this way.

Aryan had no alternative but to put them off marriage by telling them the truth. He told them that they both are brother and sister. Rahul is probably his illegitimate son from Mandy. The law does not permit marriage between a brother and a sister. Sameera had a nervous breakdown and Rahul left the house in a rage and went straight to his mother to find out the truth about him being illegitimate son of Aryan.

When Rahul reached home, he did not find his mum there. The woman next door informed him that Mandy had suffered a heart attack and was taken to the hospital in an emergency. He rushed to the hospital. She was in the intensive care unit. Her condition was quite serious. Rahul was not allowed to disturb her as she was heavily sedated with morphine. Rahul felt helpless and telephoned Aryan to come and see his mother as she was probably on her deathbed. Aryan who hated Mandy so much, was now confronted with the dilemma whether or not to go and see her.

He finally decided to see her because she was the only legitimate source to learn from, the truth about Rahul. When Aryan reached hospital, Mandy's condition had worsened. Knowing that Aryan was a well known heart surgeon, the attending doctor and Rahul requested Aryan if he would consider performing coronary bypass surgery to save Mandy. Aryan agreed and after successful surgery, when Mandy came round and opened her eyes, she thanked Aryan for saving her life. Mandy then requested Rahul to bring a black diary from the bedside table in her room.

Rahul duly brought the diary from the house. She took out a buff coloured envelope from it and handed it to Aryan to read. It said:

"Aryan I have always loved you. Not for your money but truly with my heart and soul. You were always a playboy and were never serious about our relationship. I mistook your friendship as love for me but later realised that you only enjoyed my company as no more than a good friend.

It so happened that one Christmas eve I was introduced to Tom by one of my work colleagues. We liked each other. He was a freelance artist. This was the common ground of interest between us but neither of us fancied having any close relationship. I had done some paintings and Tom promised to help me exhibit them in an art gallery. He shrewdly acted as my mentor and started visiting my flat frequently on the pretext of discussing my paintings. One evening in quite an unguarded moment, when I had a drink too many, that I gave in myself to him. When I got up in the morning Tom was gone forever.

On the other hand Aryan you have always been a perfect gentleman and never crossed the line. I now categorically admit that we had never had any sexual relationship. When I heard that you have brought Seema as you wife from India, I was very upset and hurt. I was very jealous of your marriage to Seema and since I was pregnant, I tried to extort some money from you by way of blackmail. Still you acted as a perfect gentleman by giving me the money even though you were not altogether convinced that my pregnancy was because of you.

Aryan I cashed your cheque solely for the education of Rahul and as you can see it has brought its dividends. I am happy that my son Rahul loves your daughter Sameera."

Mandy made a full recovery in a few weeks after the heart operation. Seema and Aryan came to see her at home. Mandy was delighted to welcome them and was happy to learn that Rahul had proposed to Sameera for marriage.

The morning was beautiful: there was sunshine, spring in the air and birds were singing. Aryan Seema and Mandy started preparations for the wedding of Rahul and Sameera with great fervour.

Hatred kills. Love never dies
Such is the vast difference between the two
What is obtained by love is retained for all time
What is obtained by Hatred proves a burden in reality,
For it increases Hatred.

Mahatma Gandhi.

The Playboy

Farhan Ali was an entrepreneur and a well known industrialist in Mumbai. He had a finger in every pie. He owned a few cotton mills. He also owned a television channel which was run by his mother Nusrat Begum. His father died at a young age in an accident. Nusrat Begum had brought him up alone and he was now at the peak of his career. He was married and had a ten year old daughter. He was very attached to his daughter Ruhi. His younger brother Mushtaq Ali was in charge of one of the cotton mills.

Farhan Ali had an opulent house in a posh area of south Mumbai. Mumbai formerly known as Bombay is the capital city of Maharashtra. It is the most populous in India and the fourth most populous city in the world with a total metropolitan population of more than twenty million. Besides being the wealthiest city in India, it is also the commercial and entertainment capital of India. The city houses Reserve Bank of India, Bombay Stock Exchange and of course the so called Bollywood where most of Indian movies are made.

He was on his way home from work feeling very cheerful after inspecting one of his factories that day. The factory was doing well and showed good returns. It was also his birthday. He was only forty years old and had achieved so much that many people envied him. As soon as he reached home, he was greeted by his wife Samina at the door. He was pleasantly surprised to see that the whole family had gathered together to felicitate him on his birthday. Samina, had arranged a special meal and a birthday cake.

He was very pleased to share the birthday with the whole family and after a delicious dinner, he cut the cake and gave a piece each to his mother, wife, daughter Ruhi and his brother Mushtaq. He then made a short speech thanking God for giving him such a wonderful family, specially his wife who was the driving force behind his success and his mother for having looked after him since he was a small child and helping him with his business empire.

Afterwards Farhan Ali told his wife and mother that he was going to his office to pray in a specially created prayer room, where he prayed once a week for most of the night and often returned home in early hours of the morning. When he reached office, Anar, his girlfriend was already there along with other friends, with whiskey, wine and other drinks. His wife and mother were oblivious to this dark secret of his life. At home he was a happily married man with no drinking and no smoking. Here he was having fun with his friends, drinks and girls. Anar was his special inamorata who also used to help by luring other girls for him. He had employed a number of female staff in his office and had managed to bed most of the pretty girls one way or the other. Anar managed to get girls for him either by enticing them with lots of money or intimidating them into submission because of his power and resources. Farhan Ali had several of police officials in his pay and therefore would not think twice before arrogantly flouting the law. Nobody dared complain against him.

This was however about to change soon and Farhan was in for a surprise when he reached his office the next morning. Walking towards his cabin, an attractive new girl working behind a computer caught his eye. He just could not take his eyes off her. He literally banged his head against the cabin door because his eyes were transfixed at the girl, and he did not see the cabin door. He buzzed his secretary from his office. The secretary came running to Farhan Ali. He asked about the new girl. She told him that her name is Farzana Khan and his mother Nusrat Begum had recruited her to anchor the regular chat show on their television channel. Apparently she was a very successful anchor in a rival channel and hailed as the next big thing on Indian television with her penchant for tenaciously inquisitive and probing interviews. She had achieved so much so young that Farhan Ali's mother had poached her to help boost the flagging popularity of their channel.

Farhan Ali was totally smitten with Farzana and could hardly wait. After signing some important documents, he asked for Farzana to come to his cabin. Farzana sat down in a chair opposite Farhan. He asked her the usual questions about her family and her qualifications. She told him that she lives with her mother in a flat in Bandra area in Mumbai and had done PhD in journalism. Farhan then suddenly asked her whether she would like to go out for dinner with him in the evening. Farzana was taken aback but politely declined, informing him that she had a boyfriend and was not interested in any other relationship. Farhan persisted saying that he usually takes a new girl out with a view to knowing more about her. Farzana replied that she was well aware of his reputation and about his many affairs and was not willing to go out with him. At this point she got up to leave his office. Farhan jumped out of his seat and blocking her way, grabbed hold of her and tried to molest her. But Farzana would have none of it and slapped him hard across his face and came out of his office in a rage.

Nobody had ever refused Farhan's advances till today and he was livid with a red face. Everybody in the office heard the loud slapping noise and also saw the angry face of Farzana. No one had ever dared to or dreamt of doing such a thing to Farhan before. Farhan vowed to avenge this insult. He started plotting immediately and phoned Anar who always abetted him in his dirty work. He wanted to know everything about Farzana. It was out of question for him to even contemplate sacking Farzana because she was recruited by his mother.

Anar gathered all the information about Farzana Khan in few days. He was stunned by the information Anar had unearthed. Farzana was going out with his brother Mushtaq Ali and her mother Marina Khan was a school teacher. Nobody knew about her father but there was a rumour that she was an illegitimate daughter of a minister. This gave him adequate ammunition in plotting a devious plan for his vile reprisals against Farzana.

A few days later, one evening Farhan turned up at Farzana's house and rang the doorbell. Farzana was infuriated at seeing him at her doorstep. He explained that he had come to apologise for his behaviour and to meet her mother. Farzana let him in. Her mother Marina Khan greeted him and thanked him for employing Farzana and hoped that she would prove to be an asset to his company. Farhan nodded saying that she was a very promising and hard working girl and a very popular anchor in his channel.

Farhan then told Marina Khan that he had come with a specific purpose. As his brother Mushtaq loved her daughter Farzana, he was here to ask her permission for them to get married. Marina Khan said that she will have to discuss this with Farzana and let him know. He agreed but requested that while they were mulling over the propostion, would they mind coming to his house the following week on Sunday for dinner and to meet his family. Marina Khan agreed in principle. Farhan gave them the address and phone number and after apologising again to Farzana, left their flat.

When Farhan left, Marina asked Farzana for her views about Mushtaq. She told her mother that they had been going out for two years but had not thought about marriage yet. Marina asked her whether there was any harm in meeting the family. Farzana had no issues with that. Marina Khan telephoned Farhan and confirmed that they would come to his house on Sunday week to meet the family and have dinner with them. Farhan thanked her adding that he was very pleased and looked forward to meeting them at his flat.

Farhan immediately went into action and made an insidious plan with Anar to fulfill his revenge. He wanted to kill two birds with one stone. Firstly he definitely did not want his brother to marry Farzana. He wanted to discredit Farzana by showing to his brother that she was a cheap girl, not worthy of him. Secondly he will take his revenge for his insult in the way he wanted to by satisfying his lust.

Farhan owned many flats. He had invited Marina and Farzana to one of those flats and not to his own house. His mother, wife and his brother knew nothing about this visit by Farzana and her mother. When Marina and Farzana arrived at the flat, he welcomed them at the door and ushered them inside where Anar was already present. The flat was well decorated with fresh flowers on the table. He introduced Anar to them as his wife and told them that his mother and brother were on their way. Meanwhile Anar brought drinks to them which had been spiked. Within few minutes both Marina and Farzana felt dizzy and tipsy and hardly in a state to know what was going on. Anar quickly applied a cheap and meretricious make up on both of them and Farhan then took them to a local dancing club with the help of his assistants.

Farhan then went on and actioned his second part of the plan. He phoned his brother Mushtaq Ali to come and meet him at the club. Mushtaq asked Farhan why he was calling him there. Farhan replied that a surprise awaited him there. Mushtaq agreed and set off on his way to the club.

When Mushtaq reached there, he saw Farzana and his mother in the garish make up and dancing away with different men who were all of course Farhan's people. Mushtaq was disgusted and felt very sick at seeing this and stormed out of the club and drove away. Farhan was very pleased with this desired effect it had on his brother and now went into third line of action.

He ordered two of his assistants to bring both Marina and Farzana back to his flat. He left Marina in the sitting room downstairs on the sofa, where she was still very groggy and half asleep. He took Farzana upstairs in the bedroom with the help of one of his assistants. He told his assistants to keep an eye on Marina downstairs while he completed his revenge on Farzana. He raped Farzana, who was so heavily drugged that she was in no position to resist or fight.

The last act Farhan performed was to ask his henchmen to take Farzana and Marina in the van and dump them in some deserted part of city in the early hours of morning. He rewarded his goons with a lot of money for helping him complete the revenge. His goons took both the mother and daughter in their van, drove to an isolated place and literally threw them out of the van.

Farzana was the first to regain the consciousness first and realised that her mother had hit her head on the concrete road and was bleeding profusely. She managed to call an ambulance and accompanied her to a local hospital. Doctors tried hard to revive her but she had sustained a serious head injury and had lost a lot of blood and did not survive. Farzana was devastated and distraught. Her mother's death made Farzana even more resolute and she decided to fight back. Her main priority at that point in time though was to have her mother buried first. She contacted an undertaker, who helped move her mother's body to the graveyard. After the interment of her mother she went to report the incident to police.

When she reached Bandra police station and asked the local police inspector to register her complaint and F.I.R (First Information Report). Inspector asked her;

"Madam, what is your complaint?"

"Rape and murder," Farzana replied.

"Madam, who is the person you want to register the complaint against."

"I want to register the complaint against Farhan Ali."

"Are you sure madam, you know how powerful a man he is."

"Yes I know that and I want you to write the F.I.R against him," replied Farzana

"No madam I cannot do it, I risk losing my job if I file a complaint against him," replied the police inspector unashamedly. Obviously he was on the payroll of Farhan Ali. Farzana came out of the police station very disappointed and exasperated. She saw no point in living like this.

Farzana wanted to end her life. She was left all alone in this wide world and very bewildered. Earlier at the police station a journalist, Manoj, who was present there overheard her conversation with the police inspector. Manoj came over and talked to Farzana and asked her to be patient and he will show her the way to fight back with Farhan Ali. He suggested she accompany him to his house where they will work out a plan together to make Farhan Ali pay for her humiliation and the murder of her mother. She hesitantly agreed.

Farzana went with Manoj to his house. His mother was not at all pleased that he had brought her to their house. Manoj explained that she has had a lot of problems and was in a dire need of practical as well as moral support. The mother agreed to let Farzana stay with them only till her problems were resolved. Farzana and Manoj discussed the issue through the whole night. Manoj conceded that it would not be an easy task to pick a direct fight against such a powerful man as Farhan Ali but there were hardly any other options. He also cautioned her that her honour was at stake and she should be prepared to accept the mud which would be splashed and thrown at her character. Farzana said that she was up for that and wanted to fight for her rights.

They decided that as Farzana was an anchor in the television channel she should try to get the channel to contact the Maharashtra state Home Minister Mr. Shahnawaz, who was the minister responsible for law and order in the state and interview him regarding refusal to record complaints lodged at the police stations and registering F.I.R.s. Manoj also mentioned that he could assist by calling up the Minister's secretary and seek an appointment for the interview at the channel.

Manoj had worked for the same channel in the past and personally knew Farhan's mother Nusrat Begum, who was in charge of the chat show. Manoj went over to Nusrat Begum and suggested that if they could interview Home Minister Shahnawaz. She asked if there was any particular reason for an interview with Shahnawaz. Manoj said that there had been lots of complaints by ordinary citizens that the police were not registering complaints and also had refused to register any F.I.Rs in many cases. Nusrat Begum gave permission to Manoj to arrange an interview and let know Farzana Khan.

Manoj succeeded in getting an early date and time fixed for the interview with Shahnawaz Khan and advised Farzana to prepare her interview questions. When Farhan got wind of this, he suggested to his mother that the interview should not take place on their channel. His mother rejected his suggestion and said that it was a topical and public issue which will be of immense interest to the viewership and will go a long way towards boosting the popularity of their channel. Besides, Farzana was an excellent anchor and would handle it well.

Farhan felt very uneasy. Shahnawaz was actually his father-in-law. He decided to go and see him to dissuade him from appearing for this interview. Shahnawaz did not wish to cancel the interview. He said to Farhan that with elections looming for the state assembly, he did not want to miss out on this opportunity of free publicity. Farhan then suggested an alternative option that he will write certain answers to probable questions and the minister should stay around those answers during the interview. Shahnawaz said that whilst he will try to do so, he could not give any firm undertaking that he will strictly adhere to his predetermined answers.

Meanwhile Farzana tried to contact her boyfriend Mushtaq on the phone but he was very angry and did not want to meet her. Farzana asked him the reason to which he said that she was such a cheap and frivolous girl that he did not want to keep any relations with her. This made Farzana more upset. She was not aware that Mushtaq had seen her in a dancing club in that tawdry make up and in a drunken state. The dirty trick by Farhan Ali had paid off.

Anyway Farzana did not lose courage. She soldiered on with the help of journalist Manoj and prepared the questions for the interview with the Home Minister. At the appointed date and time Home Minister Shahnawaz arrived at the studio. It was a live interview at peak viewing time in the evening and was heavily advertised. A very large number of viewers were expected to watch this programme and Farzana asked very tough and searching questions regarding law and order alluding to refusal by the police force to register F.I.R complaints. Predictably the minister like any other politician asked if she could furnish an example of F.I.R complaint and cite the police department that had refused to register complaints. To which Farzana replied that provided he was prepared to give an undertaking here and now that he would take an appropriate action, she would name the person and the police station where the complaint was refused. The minister agreed and said he will not hesitate in taking action. Farzana said that she will hold him to his promise as millions of viewers were watching. Shahnawaz gave her his word of honour.

The minister was astounded when Farzana told him that she herself was the victim of a recent rape and had tried to register an F.I.R at Bandra police station which was refused point blank. Minister found it incredible that a sophisticated woman like Farzana would declare herself to be a rape victim in front of millions of viewers. But he had to accept that it must be the truth for Farzana to risk disgracing herself openly on the television. Shahnawaz promised a crackdown on this malpractice of failure to register any F.I.R complaints, without exception, by the police force in Mumbai. He warned of severe disciplinary action against any police officer found in breach of his duties. Minister emerged out of the studio visibly very upset and with a disdainful look on his face.

Farhan Ali watched the interview and felt ill at ease. He leaked a bombshell to the media that Farzana Khan was the illegitimate daughter of Shahnawaz Khan. He again wanted to kill two birds with one stone. Listening to this news Shahnawaz will not dare proceed with the crackdown on the police and Farzana will not persist with rape charges against him.

This had the desired effect. Shahnawaz Khan was mobbed by press on his way home. They wanted to know the truth whether Farzana was his daughter or not. He denied outright that Farzana was his daughter. When pressed further Shahnawaz made no further comments.

Deep down though Shahnawaz had an instinctive feeling that Farzana was his daughter. Farzana's mother Marina Khan was the younger sister of his wife. His wife suffered from cancer and was unable to look after their baby daughter Samina. Marina Khan came over to stay with them to look after the little child. As his wife spent a great deal of time in the hospital due to her illness he had gradually developed intimate relations with Marina Khan. After some time Marina Khan became pregnant and implored Shahnawaz that he should marry her but Shahnawaz did not agree as his wife was still alive. He could ill afford any scandal, being a public figure. Marina Khan moved out from his house and gave birth to a little baby girl who she named Farzana. Marina Khan cared for and raised Farzana alone as a single parent. Farzana knew all about this and despised Shahnawaz for it.

After the television interview Shahnawaz went over to see Farzana but she was too consternated to listen to him and said that she loathed him. He said that he was very sorry that her mother had suffered because of him but now he wanted to make amends and give her the emotional support especially as she had been a rape victim. She replied that she was quite capable of looking after herself provided the police acted dutifully and registered her F.I.R. It was now up to him to keep his promise and issue instructions to all police stations to register complaints from general public and take appropriate action. He affirmed that he will certainly do that and will only be too happy to help with any other support she needed. Farzana thanked him for that.

Mushtaq Ali came to see Farzana after the interview at the television studio. Farzana was very incensed that just when she needed his support the most, he had turned his back on her. She felt betrayed and deeply hurt. Mushtaq pleaded with her but she refused to meet him. Despite Mushtaq's repeated apologies to her, she would not budge and showed him the door. When Farzana had finished for the night and left the studio for home Mushtaq followed her to her house. He rang the doorbell but Farzana shut the door in his face as soon as she saw him. It kept raining the whole night and when Farzana opened her front door at dawn for the morning paper she found Mushtaq lying outside fully drenched and soaking wet. She felt compassionate towards him and brought him inside.

Farzana could see, that he was dishevelled and in a sorry state suffering from cold and sleep deprivation. She gave him a towel and some dry clothes and asked him to tidy himself up while she made him a hot cup of tea and some breakfast. After Mushtaq had the hot drink and food and regained his composure somewhat, Farzana recounted her ordeal to him. How his brother Farhan Ali had duped her and her mother to get them to his flat, instead of his house, where he had drugged them and took them to some squalid dancing club in a raffish and gaudy make up and then back to his flat where he raped her. And all this was because she had slapped Farhan in his office for his sleazy advances.

Mushtaq now felt compelled to believe every word of her story and said that his brother had played a similar trick on him and called him to the dancing club to show her and her mother in a vile and gross makeover and in an inebriated state. Mushtaq found Farhan's actions disgustingly abhorrent for the way, his brother wanted him to break his relationship with Farzana. Mushtaq vowed that he will back Farzana wholeheartedly in her efforts to lay bare the sadistic violence perpetrated on her by his own brother. Farzana felt very much upbeat with this moral support from Mushtaq.

She went to Bandra police station the next day and registered an F.I.R against Farhan Ali. The police inspector could not refuse this time as explicit instructions had been issued by the Home Minister to record all complaints against anybody however powerful the person, against whom the complaint is made, may be. The news of the rape case against Farhan Ali spread like wildfire through all the media. Every newspaper and television channel wanted to interview Farhan Ali about this allegation. Farhan Ali declined to comment but issued a statement that he will file a lawsuit against Farzana for defamation.

When minister Shahnawaz heard these allegations, he went to his son-in-law Farhan Ali's house and launched into a tirade at him. Farhan Ali vehemently denied that he had anything to do with the rape.

Shahnawaz did not believe a word Farhan Ali said and kept yelling at him and accused him of ruining Farzana's life. Much finger-wagging and recriminations ensued between the father-in-law and the son-in-law. Suddenly Farhan asked Shahnawaz that was it not true that Farzana was his illegitimate daughter and was it not the reason for his aggressive behaviour.

Shahnawaz had to admit that Farzana was his daughter. Hearing that, Farhan Ali burst into sarcastic laughter and chided, "go away and look after your illegitimate daughter whom you had abandoned years ago." Shahnawaz became very agitated at hearing this and took out a hand gun and aimed at Farhan. Hearing their heated altercation Farhan's mother Nusrat Begum and wife Samina came rushing in from the adjoining room and intervened to prevent Shahnawaz from shooting Farhan. Shahnawaz left in a huff and while leaving, said that he will do everything in his power to help Farzana.

As soon as Shahnawaz left Farhan's house, Nusrat Begum and Samina confronted Farhan regarding the rape allegation of Farzana. Farhan repudiated the rape charge and said that it was a totally baseless allegation. His wife pressed him further to take an oath of honour on his daughter's life. He took the false oath without any hesitation and again reiterated that he had nothing to do with the rape. Samina was unsettled on coming to know that her father Shahnawaz had an affair and Farzana was her illegitimate half-sister. Farhan then asked his mother Nusrat Begum to sack Farzana but his mother did not agree as she thought that it might make matters worse.

Shahnawaz Khan got home very upset. He realised that he had neglected his daughter Farzana all these years and now was his chance to make up for the lost time. He telephoned Mushtaq Ali and asked him if he would marry his daughter Farzana. Shahnawaz undertook to provide all the financial backing and moral support.

Mushtaq Ali assured Shahnawaz that he was deeply in love with Farzana and would do everything to help her recover from this traumatic phase in her life.

Shahnawaz Khan now though somewhat relieved about Farzana was still under a lot of stress, because the media will hound him when they come to learn that Farzana was indeed his illegitimate daughter. His reputation and political career were at stake. This is how the events that followed, unfolded. As soon as he came out of the house in his official car, the media lay in wait to quiz him about Farzana. He refused to comment but media people were persistent and blocked the way of his car. In his state of extreme stress he suffered a stroke with loss of speech. The chauffeur took him to Breach Candy hospital where doctors found him with the left side of his body paralysed. Doctors were very doubtful of his early recovery. With the loss of his speech, he was unable to say or instruct anything. It was very sad because he was in no state now to provide any help and support to Farzana.

Farhan Ali went to offer his sympathies to his father-in-law Shahnawaz in the hospital but within his heart he breathed a sigh of relief that Shahnawaz cannot now help Farzana and even hoped the police might drop all charges against him. He had the audacity to call up Farzana suggesting that she withdrew her case against him or else he himself would file a case of defamation against her. But Farzana was determined to go ahead with her action against him for her humiliation. Farhan menacingly told her that he had a lot of influence with judges in the court and she will never win any case against him. Farhan then asked his brother Mushtaq to come back home because Farzana had made false allegations against him. Mushtaq remained adamant that he will not come home because he believed in Farzana's story and he felt deep revulsion towards him for spoiling Farzana's life. He was very much in love with Farzana and vowed to stand by her always.

The rape case of Farzana was heard in the court and as expected Farhan used his influence and money to buy out the judge. In spite of all the efforts of Farzana, Mushtaq and Manoj the all-too-predictable result of the case being dismissed was announced by the court. The rape charge could not be proved against Farhan. Farzana of course was very disappointed and depressed. She wanted to appeal in the higher court but was not sure whether she will be able to win the case as Farhan will use the same tactics to counter her appeal as well.

Farhan was very pleased with himself. He had won the case and now he wanted to celebrate. He phoned his wife Samina that he was going to his prayer room to thank God for his success. In fact he was going to celebrate with his cronies and Anar in his special drinking and smoking room at his office. He and his friends revelled in a binge drinking and eating well into the night. He returned home in the early hours of the morning.

At home his wife Samina was still awake with his daughter Ruhi complaining of severe headache. Ruhi was in distress, crying and holding her head. Ruhi was Farhan's pet little girl and he doted on her. He could not bear to see his child suffering like this. He decided to take her to hospital.

At the hospital the doctors examined Ruhi and told Farhan that she needed MRI (Magnetic Resonance Image) scan to determine the cause of her severe headache. MRI scan was done in the morning which indicated that Ruhi had a brain cancer. Farhan was shattered. He could not bear to see his little girl Ruhi in such pain. No medicine was able to reduce her pain.

Farhan, his wife Samina and mother Nusrat Begum consulted a noted cancer specialist and neurologist who too did not hold out much hope for Ruhi's survival. The specialist also told them that she had an inoperable cancer and she may not survive for long. All three stayed around Ruhi's bed round the clock taking in turns so that one of them was with Ruhi all the time. Farhan felt very frustrated and helpless seeing Ruhi suffer like this but for all the wealth he possessed he could do nothing to help. Mushtaq Ali came to see his niece at the hospital when he heard of her illness. Farhan would not let him see Ruhi. He curtly told him to go away and canoodle with Farzana. He did not want to see him anymore. Mushtaq was very upset that he could not see his favourite niece and he was turned away from hospital by his mother Nusrat Begum as well.

Ruhi did not survive more than forty eight hours. When Farhan Ali buried her at the graveyard, he could not hold back his tears. He knew that all his life he had done so many wrong things. He felt guilt-ridden and blamed himself as being solely responsible for Ruhi's death. He had taken a false oath on her life. God had punished him for his misdeeds.

Farhan's mother and wife accused him of taking a false oath on Ruhi's life and held him responsible for her death at such a young and tender age. They told him that he should come clean and tell the truth. Farhan's conscience kept pricking him. He knew that he was in the wrong and it was time that he told the truth. He promised his mother and wife that he will try to make a clean breast of it and tell the whole world about all his past indiscretions and evil ways.

Next afternoon he came live on his own channel and remorsefully owned up to all his misdemeanours.

He said in his speech:

"I admit that all my life I have been a playboy and have had sexual relationship with many girls. Most girls invariably gave in, because of my power and were apprehensive of complaining against me. I have many people working for me who would intimidate the girls into submission. I confess that I had raped Farzana Khan for revenge because she was the only one ever to refuse me and who slapped me in the face in front of my staff. I also admit that I was the main person responsible for the death of Farzana's mother Marina Khan."

He went on to confess that he had knowingly taken a false oath on his daughter's life and believed it was God's way of punishing him by taking away his much loved daughter Ruhi from him.

He conceded that he had led a duplicitous, caddish and pathetic life. At home he pretended he was a God fearing man with no vices. Away from his home, he indulged in binge drinking, risqué parties and wild orgies ensuring his wife and mother never came to know anything about it.

He concluded by apologising to Farzana Khan and his brother Mushtaq Ali for his iniquities and wished them well and was happy for his brother to marry Farzana Khan.

Suddenly Farhan Ali burst into a bout of loud boisterous laughter. The TV presenter hastily pulled the plug and went off air. The perplexed presenter did her best to calm Farhan down but no avail. When his guffaw continued unabated, the presenter called her boss.

Nusrat Begum arrived accompanied by Samina. They too were baffled to see the state he was in and by his buffoonish behaviour. With the help of their chauffeur they took him to the car park and hurriedly escorted him home. Before long, the police arrived at Farhan's house with a warrant for his arrest on multiple charges. Despite Nusrat Begum's pleas to the police to wait while she called her lawyer, the inspector insisted on taking Farhan Ali into custody. Much to everyone's surprise, fascinated by the flashing lights of the police van waiting outside, Farhan Ali ran out and jumped into the van like a small child before the police could put the hand cuffs on him. Nusrat Begum helplessly watched them drive off.

First thing next morning Nusrat Begum and Samina accompanied by their lawyers arrived at the police station for legal representation of Farhan Ali's case. They were informed that during the interrogation overnight, Farhan behaved strangely laughing and crying at the same time. The officer on duty immediately referred him for psychiatric assessment to the Mental Health Department of Mumbai police. Just then the news came that Farhan Ali had been certified as mentally unstable and not in control of his actions, in other words he was declared insane. He had been admitted to the mental hospital for treatment and further investigation. Meanwhile the police department obtained court orders which stated that if there were to be no noticeable improvement in his mental condition in the next three months, he will be transferred to languish in a lunatic asylum for the rest of his days or until the hearing in court if he got better, where if convicted of rape and murder he faced a mandatory life term to rot in prison.

Was this a fitting end of the Playboy? Only time will tell...

As soon as we lose the moral basis,
We cease to be religious.
There is no such thing as religion
Over-riding morality
Man, for instance,
Cannot be untruthful,
Cruel or incontinent
And claim
To have God on his side.

Mahatma Gandhi

Sins of The Soul

Imtiaz Ahmed lived with his wife Fatima and two daughters, Sakina thirteen years and Ambreen seven in Hazratganj town of Lucknow, in northern India. He joined the family business run by his father who was a plumber by trade and owned a hardware shop. After Imtiaz's father died the responsibility of looking after all the members of his family fell squarely upon his shoulders. His younger brother Rafiq, who always had a divisive streak in his nature, was not much help to him in the business. Every now and then he would have an argument regarding his share of property and business which their father had left behind.

Unfortunately the mother always sided with her younger son. It became difficult for Imtiaz to continue living together in such acrimonious joint family. He therefore decided to move away with his wife and two girls to another town called Amethi. The inheritance was divided among the members of the family in accordance with Muslim law. With whatever he got from the ancestral inheritance as his share Imtiaz started his own hardware business but he had to face a lot of difficulties because of the lack of adequate financial resources. He soldiered on with diligence, nevertheless.

Fatima, Imtiaz's wife backed up her husband with her share of support during that difficult period. She was good at stitching clothes and embroidery work. She bought a sewing machine and started working as seamstress from home. During Eid and Diwali she could earn well. Her contribution to their family income turned out to be of great help. The girls were growing up and went to a local school.

Imtiaz's mother was getting on in years and had become frail and infirm with ill health. One day the news came that she died of heart attack. Imtiaz and his wife rushed to pay their last respects to the departed soul and be with the grieving family. Imtiaz's quarrelsome brother Rafiq imperiously made a lot of fuss and created a row. He just did not want them there. He was afraid that Imtiaz might demand his share in the assets left behind by their mother. But Imtiaz was least interested in it. He quietly went his way after performing the last rites of his mother.

The time passed by. Imtiaz and his wife were happily and steadily going through the ups and downs confronted in day to day's survival. The elections were soon to take place throughout the country. The election campaign was in full swing. Communal riots broke out during that time much to Imtiaz's despair. A curfew was imposed in the town which went on for ten days and affected his business immensely. It so happened that during the riots his shop was vandalised and looted by some miscreants. This was a great setback to his means of survival. His family suffered a great deal of hardship.

Imtiaz struggled to make both ends meet. Good jobs were scarce and he found it very hard meeting the ever increasing expenses of running his household and education of his daughters. Some of his friends who had been to Dubai were able to earn much more than they did in India and regularly sent their savings back home to their families so that they were able to sustain a reasonable standard of living. One of his friends Farid had just returned to India with a huge sum of money earned in Dubai and had set up his own business in India.

Imtiaz went to meet Farid who suggested that he should also go to Dubai where he will earn more money than he did here. He too could send his savings to his family in India, which will greatly help run the household and ensure that his daughters continued to receive good education. Imtiaz discussed the venture of going to Dubai with his wife, who was quite apprehensive at first but later agreed in principle provided that it was for a limited period of few years and not indefinitely. She added that so long as he also visited the family back home twice a year, she was happy for him to give it a try in Dubai.

Though not altogether happy to leave his wife and daughters behind on their own, Imtiaz took that painful decision for the sake of better and secure future for his family.

Imtiaz got his passport and visa ready and went to an agent who used to arrange work permits for Dubai. It was not too difficult in his case as Dubai needed skilled manpower and Imtiaz was a good plumber, though he had to pay a heavy commission to the agent to hurry the process up which is quite normal in India. It took about six months and Imtiaz arrived in Dubai.

Imtiaz landed at the Dubai International airport. He was very impressed by the airport and was fascinated by the information given about it. Spread over an area of 8460 acres of land Dubai airport is the 4th busiest airport in the world. It is an important contributor to the economy employing 58000 people and supporting 25000 jobs in Dubai. It contributes over US $22 billion to Dubai's economy.

Imtiaz was met by his employer's agent, who escorted him to a dormitory type of accommodation. On the way to his lodgings the agent gave him brief history of Dubai. The earliest mention of Dubai is in 1905 AD. Its strategic geographical location made the town an important trading hub for the region and by the beginning of the 20th century Dubai became an important regional port. Today Dubai has emerged as a cosmopolitan metropolis and has grown to become a global city.

Although Dubai's economy is built on oil industry, its western-style model of business brings main revenue from tourism, real estate, and financial services. It has many skyscrapers and high-rise buildings including the world's tallest building Burj Khalifa, several man made islands, hotels and shopping malls. Dubai is the 22nd most expensive city in the world surpassing London. It has been rated as one of the best places to live in the Middle East.

The dormitory where the agent took him was not a great place but a very small flat where a lot of migrant workers were put up in. The flat consisted of one big hall, a kitchen, toilet and a bathroom. In the hall there were four beds laid down on the floor. There were three occupants. Imtiaz was the fourth one to join the team of workers. He was introduced to Ramnathan who was from Sri Lanka, another one came from Punjab in Pakistan called Mola Jat. The third occupant, Babu Bhai was from Mumbai.

They all welcomed the new arrival. It took some time for Imtiaz to get familiar with them, but once they got to know each other they became very close. He soon got to know all about the required work of the company which had employed him. There was never a day when he did not think of his wife and children. Friday was a day off for all workers and he always made it a point to call up his family in India for a weekly chat.

After a few months he got well acquainted with the social and cultural events which took place in Dubai. He used to attend the functions of Hindu festivals with Ramnathan. On Eid, with other flat mates there was lots of cooking, eating and revelry.

It was tough going in the beginning but his earnings were good and he was able to send regular remittances to his wife for the housekeeping and the education of his daughters. At the end of one year, he was able to visit his family in Amethi and happy to tell them that it was going swimmingly for him in Dubai. His wife was also quite relieved to see him earning more money in Dubai but she did feel lonely without him. He promised that he will return as soon as he had earned enough money to start his own business in India. Fatima seemed satisfied with his promise and eagerly awaited the day when he will come back to India for good.

Babu Bhai became Imtiaz's great pal and confidant. Imtiaz confided in him about most of his anxieties and problems. Babu Bhai was a rough person in behavior but had a heart of gold and always ready to help others time of need. It was nearly the end of Imtiaz's four year contract. He had now saved quite a substantial sum of money. He had lots of dreams for a better life in India, after finishing his contract in Dubai.

Back home in India Sakina the eldest daughter would often run errands for her mother like fetching grocery from the corner shop whenever her mother ran short of certain provisions. Sakina was a very attractive girl with lots of boys after her but she did not want to have anything to do with them. She had higher ambitions and wanted to choose the boy herself. One day her mother asked her to get some rice. When she went to the corner shop, the usual shopkeeper was away and his son Javed was there instead looking after the shop. Javed told her that his father was unwell hence he was managing the shop. When Sakina tried to pay for the rice Javed declined to accept and asked her if she would go out in the evening with him. Sakina was incensed, threw the money in his face and slapped him hard in front of all the people present in the shop.

Javed was very upset and could not swallow this public humiliation. He vowed that he would take revenge on Sakina for it. No girl had ever refused or insulted him before like this. He conspired with two of his friends Sarfraz and Mohsin with whom he usually hung around, to avenge his humiliation whenever an opportunity came his way. Sakina returned home in a rage but refrained from telling her mother about this incident. She did not want to worry her mother while her father was away. It probably would have made her mother even more furious and she would have called up her father in Dubai and he would have been very infuriated as well. However this incident was to result in consequences so grave that nobody expected.

It so happened that a few weeks later, one evening Fatima had run out of potatoes and cooking oil. As Sakina was preoccupied with her exams, she sent her younger daughter Ambreen to get the stuff from the corner shop. When Ambreen reached the shop, she found it closed but Javed was still there who suggested that she went with him to their other shop a little further away where she will be able to get her groceries.

Ambreen was an innocent and a naive young girl, barely eleven years old and readily accompanied him. On the way he texted his mates Mohsin and Sarfraz to join him. Together all three took Ambreen to a disused barn where they sexually assaulted her. It was horrible. Poor girl screamed and screamed for help but nobody came to her rescue. It was a barbaric and inhuman act to rape an innocent girl of eleven, all because her elder sister had refused to go out with Javed. The three boys took off after committing this heinous act, leaving Ambreen behind bleeding and unconscious.

Meanwhile at home, Fatima was beginning to get worried as Ambreen had been gone over an hour and should have been well back by now. Fatima went out looking for her at the corner store but found it closed. She looked around but there was no sign of Ambreen. She decided to go to the police and report Ambreen missing. The police inspector was very sympathetic especially when he came to know that the missing person was a minor girl. Realising the gravity of situation he sent two of his experienced officers to look out for Ambreen. Soon afterwards the policemen found her in the abandoned barn in a very bad state and rushed her to the local hospital and informed her mother.

The doctor who examined her found that Ambreen had been sexually assaulted by more than one person. She had lost a lot of blood and was still unconscious. When Fatima reached the hospital the doctor explained the whole situation telling her that it may take few weeks for Ambreen to recover from the shock. The doctor also reported the matter to police and informed them that Ambreen may take some time to regain consciousness, before she would be able to answer any of their questions in establishing the identity the culprits. The police inspector asked Fatima whether she suspected anybody. Fatima was unable to help police with their inquiries except for telling them that she had sent Ambreen to fetch some groceries from the corner shop.

Javed, Mohsin and Sarfraz left Amethi for their college next day. All three of them used to stay in a hostel near the college. They had come to know that Ambreen was admitted to hospital in an unconscious state. They did not want to be around when she regained her consciousness. She was still in a bad shape and the doctor told the family that she needed to remain in the hospital till she recovered completely. Ambreen was having nightmares and was not in a fit state of mind. The hospital psychologist was counselling her and trying to get her out from the ordeal she had been through.

It was middle of the night in Dubai and Imtiaz had just returned to his flat after completing a late shift that evening. Suddenly the telephone rang. He rushed and picked up the phone. It was his wife who had called him in the small hours of the morning. He was obviously very anxious when his wife asked him to come home to India urgently. He kept on asking what the matter was but she could hardly utter anything as she was rather tearful and trying hard to maintain her composure. She could not summon up the courage to tell him over the phone about what had happened to Ambreen. She could only keep repeating, "Please come home urgently, I beseech you and need you".

Imtiaz was torn into pieces by this phone call. He thought his daughter may be seriously ill and he needed to be with her. He woke up Babu Bhai and asked for his help and advice. Babu Bhai advised him to see his boss in the morning and ask for leave, on compassionate grounds, to go home to see his ailing daughter. If his boss tried to be difficult then Babu Bhai will try to persuade his boss to grant him some unpaid leave.

Imtiaz approached his boss the next day for a short leave, but his boss got infuriated and turned down his request. Babu Bhai however saved the situation and his boss agreed to sanction his leave only for one week on the condition that his contract will not be renewed if Imtiaz failed to come back by that period. Imtiaz had no choice but to agree to that condition. He immediately booked a flight and Babu Bhai saw him off at the airport reassuring him of all his support. Imtiaz was very grateful and hugged him very warmly. The plane took off and the tall majestic buildings of Dubai started appearing smaller and smaller as the aircraft soared into the sky. A few hours later he landed at Delhi airport. After Customs and Immigration clearances, he took a coach to his home town. When he reached home, his wife briefed him all about Ambreen. He went straight to the hospital and did his best to console his daughter.

After some four weeks Ambreen had made sufficient recovery and was discharged from the hospital. The police visited Ambreen at home the next day to ask her about the identity of the culprits. But Ambreen was so much traumatized by the nightmares that she could not remember the culprits. She also told her father that she wanted to go far away from Amethi because it reminded her of the ordeal and gave her nightmares. Imtiaz discussed the pitiable plight of his daughter with his wife who agreed that they should move to Delhi. He had made sufficient money in Dubai and informed his boss and Babu Bhai that he was not coming back to Dubai. He did not foresee any hardship in being able to move to Delhi and begin a new life there.

It took Imtiaz few months to sell the house in Amethi and move to Delhi. He rented a house around Jama Masjid area in Delhi. Imtiaz chose this area because he had a friend living there. Besides, being religious, he thought that with daily prayers in the Masjid it will give his daughter the strength and fortitude to get over the tragic incident that had befallen her. Jama Masjid is the principal mosque of Old Delhi. It was built by Mughal Emperor Shah Jahan in the year 1656 AD. It is the largest and the best-known mosque in India. The courtyard of the mosque can hold up to twenty five thousand worshippers and is generally very busy on Friday noon congregation prayers of Muslims.

Ten years went by. Imtiaz had now fully established his plumbing business. He ran a plumber's merchant shop with a few people working for him. He had a good knowledge of plumbing trade which had been enhanced further after working in Dubai. The money he saved from the house he sold in Amethi had come in very handy. His business went from strength to strength and he bought a three bedroom house in the same area. His eldest daughter Sakina completed a degree from Delhi University and became a teacher at a local school. His younger daughter Ambreen was still studying Law at a local college.

Imtiaz and Fatima were well settled in Delhi. Their priority in life now was to get both their daughters married. Imtiaz was more anxious to get Ambreen married. He discussed it with Fatima and Sakina. They both were in agreement that Ambreen should be married first having suffered the traumatic episode during her childhood. Besides, Sakina let her parents know that she liked a person named Akmal who was also a teacher at her school. However Sakina and Akmal were not quite ready to get married yet. Sakina also mentioned to her parents that Akmal had a younger brother Elias who might make a suitable match for marriage with Ambreen. Akmal had mentioned to Sakina that his brother Elias was a devout Muslim but he had a peculiar habit of washing his hands frequently for no apparent reason.

Imtiaz and Fatima were happy to know about Elias and his being very religious was actually a good thing in their view. It so happened that one day Elias saw Ambreen in one of the shopping centres in Delhi. Though he did not immediately recognise her, he seemed to think that he had seen her before somewhere. Suddenly it struck him that it was he who, along with Javed and Sarfraz, was the perpetrator of sexual violation of this girl several years ago when she was still a child. Elias's full name was Elias Mohsin

Elias became anxious to know whether Ambreen recognized him. He went over and stood next to Ambreen and waited in nervous anticipation but she did not recognize him at all. Perhaps she had not seen his face during the sexual assault because she had become unconscious at that time. Though he himself had not actually assaulted her, yet he had abetted his friends in that ghastly crime. He had restrained her by holding down her arms with his hands during that wanton act. He had felt guilt ridden ever since and sought solace by turning to religion. He had also grown a small beard. Because of his guilt Elias felt that his hands were soiled by that dirty deed and had got into this habit of washing them frequently. He desperately wanted to make amends and tried to wash away his sins.

Elias felt greatly relieved that Ambreen had not recognised him. He decided to approach her in a friendly manner to capitalize on this chance meeting. He asked Ambreen if she had finished shopping, would she mind having tea with him in a cafe at the shopping centre. Ambreen felt quite waery after shopping and Elias seemed a decent fellow to her, so she readily agreed.

During tea they started chatting. Ambreen told him all about herself and her family and that she was a law student at Delhi University. She had an elder sister Sakina who was a teacher at one of the schools in Old Delhi. Her father ran a plumbing shop near Jama Masjid. Elias told Ambreen that his father ran a clothes shop around Jama Masjid and he had an elder brother Akmal who was also a teacher at the same school as her sister's. He surmised that probably Akmal might know his sister Sakina. In spite of it being a big wide world, it still is a small place seeing how people meet each other. After tea they exchanged their contact numbers before parting and agreed to meet again.

Ambreen told her parents about her meeting with Elias and about his brother Akmal working as a teacher at the same school as Sakina. Her parents were happy because Sakina had already mentioned about Akmal and his younger brother Elias. It was a chance meeting with lot of significance.

Elias also mentioned about his meeting with Ambreen to his parents. His brother Akmal was quite delighted with this meeting between Elias and Ambreen. The parents felt relieved that at last Elias had liked some girl and he might come out of his obsessive habit of washing hands frequently. Little did they know about the guilty conscience from which Elias was suffering!

Elias did meet Ambreen again, once for dinner and again for coffee. He was quietly confident that Ambreen enjoyed his company and would be happy to marry him. He mentioned this to his parents and to his brother. Akmal had no issues with Elias marrying first. His parents also had no objection to this proposition. Elias's parents went over to meet Ambreen's parents and they were quite happy with the matrimonial proposal. One request that Ambreen's parents made was that she should finish her law degree before they got married. There was no objection from Elias's parents as Ambreen was due to finish her exams in two months time.

Two months passed very quickly. Ambreen cleared her Law degree. Everyone was pleased. Elias congratulated Ambreen on her success. Preparations for the marriage got underway in earnest on both sides. Many relatives and friends were sent invitations by both families to attend the wedding and bless the couple. Imtiaz and Fatima along with Elias's parents Samina and Sohail had agreed that they will have a simple Nikah ceremony on Saturday followed by a reception on Sunday. They also had agreed that both parties will share the total expenditure of the wedding equally.

Ambreen was given a bridal make up by a professional beautician and she looked gorgeous. Elias dressed as the groom arrived in a cream coloured sherwani. A Muslim priest was in attendance to perform the Nikah ceremony in a large hall. Lots of guests from both sides had gathered for the happy event. There was a woman from the groom's side who had come from Amethi. When this lady saw Ambreen, she kept staring at her trying hard to remember where she had seen this girl before. Suddenly it struck her that Ambreen was the girl who was raped during her childhood. She created a scene and recounted the incident to Elias's parents and vilified the bride's family. Sohail and Samina were outraged that Imtiaz and Fatima had held back this sensitive information from them.

Imtiaz and Fatima explained in their defence that they did not consider it that important and besides they did not to want to remember this traumatic episode which had made them leave Amethi. There was a fair amount of heated discussion and this marriage ceremony turned into a fiasco. Elias's parents were not prepared to go through with the Nikah ceremony and left the hall in a rage.

Imtiaz, Fatima, Sakina and Ambreen were all very distraught.

They were at a loss what to do. Ambreen was more upset than anybody else. Her wounds had been gouged open again. It had taken her all these years to forget and leave behind her childhood tragic episode and move on in her life. She went into a shell and stopped talking to anyone. Her parents tried to comfort her but she had become totally disconsolate. She went into deep depression and cocooned herself in her room. Normally the level headed Sakina too was distressed and livid at this turn of events. She suspected that perhaps now under the prevailing circumstances even Akmal might refrain from marrying her.

While in Elias's house, his parents were not sure what to do either. They wanted to get Elias married but not after knowing the childhood story of Ambreen. At this stage Akmal turned out to be the wisest person in the house. He tried to convince his parents that it was not Ambreen's fault that she had been a victim of rape. Elias also told his parents that he did not mind marrying Ambreen despite the stigma attached to her tragic past. He did not though let on his parents and brother that he himself was one of the culprits in that sadistic affair.

Elias did not have the moral courage to admit his guilt. Eventually Samina and Sohail relented realising that they have been unfair to Ambreen and her parents. They felt it was unwise of them to have paid heed to that woman from Amethi who had led them into calling off the Nikah ceremony. They went over to Imtiaz and Fatima's house and apologized for their behaviour. Imtiaz and Fatima were pleased to welcome them back in their house. They agreed that under the circumstances Samina and Sohail's reaction was understandable.

Imtiaz, Fatima, Samina and Sohail agreed to get Elias and Ambreen married in a simple Nikah ceremony this time without inviting any of their relatives and friends. They did not want any more distractions. A Nikah ceremony was performed by a Muslim priest in Imtiaz and Fatima's house. After the wedding Elias, Samina and Sohail brought Ambreen to their house. Elias and Ambreen decided to go to Shimla for honeymoon.

Shimla formerly known as Simla, is the capital city of the state

74

of Himachal Pradesh. Once the cool retreat for the colonial British it is set in the forested foothills of the Himalayas located in northern India. It is bounded by Mandi and Kullu in the north, Kinaur in the east, state of Uttaranchal in the south east and Solan and Srimaur to the south. The elevation of the city ranges from 300 to 2200 meters. Shimla is well known as a hub for Indian tourism. It is one of the top ten preferred entrepreneurial locations in India. In 1864, Simla was declared as a summer capital of British India. Its name is derived from the goddess Shyamla Devi, an incarnation of the Hindu goddess Kali.

Elias and Ambreen had booked a honeymoon suite in one of the Taj group of hotels. They reached there in the early afternoon. After lunch they went for a walk. There were lots of tourists around. Lots of people were looking at the couple. Eventually they came to a road where one man kept looking at Ambreen. Elias got very angry and got into brawl with him. Some people intervened and rescued the man from Elias's punches.

Ambreen suggested to Elias that they should go back to the hotel room. In the hotel room Ambreen asked him why he was so mad at the man. Elias said he just did not like people ogling at her. She said it was not the right thing to do and he should control his anger. People will always be around and he should be tolerant in his attitude. Elias promised that he will try to control his temper in future. The honeymoon did not go very well because Ambreen was not very responsive due to Elias's attitude and Elias too had become very jittery over even minor things. Eventually Ambreen asked Elias the reason of his attitude and anger.

Elias thought that time had now come for him to come out clean about his sordid past. He had been carrying a heavy burden on his chest since last ten years. He could not hide it anymore and told Ambreen that he was one of the boys involved in that sexual assault on her when she was a child. Though he made it clear by taking an oath with God as witness that he personally had not sexually assaulted her but felt guilty nonetheless because he did not prevent his friends from committing that horrific crime. Ambreen was outraged on hearing this and told

Elias that she wanted to go back to her parents in Delhi.

Elias and Ambreen were back in Delhi within two days. Sohail and Samina were surprised but were even more shocked when Ambreen packed her bags and left for her parents house. Samina and Sohail asked Elias what had gone wrong. Elias did not want to hide anything anymore. He confessed to his parents that years ago he was one of the culprits involved in the sexual assault on Ambreen. Though he again stressed on his parents that he himself had not assaulted her, he admitted that he had held her arms with his hands to restrain her during the attack. Ever since that fateful day he had been suffering from pangs of guilt for not having stopped his friends from committing that horrible crime. That was the main reason that he believed that his hands had become dirty and why he washed his hands frequently.

At this stage his elder brother Akmal suggested that since he has confessed about his crime to his parents and Ambreen with a clear conscience, it would be best if he went over and apologized to Ambreen with a sincere heart and plead with her to bury the past and come back to him.

Elias agreed to his advice and went over to Ambreen's house. Imtiaz and Fatima were not happy to see Elias because Ambreen had locked herself in her room and was not prepared to see anybody. Elias requested that he needed at least one chance to talk to Ambreen. They agreed and left him to talk to Ambreen. Elias spoke to Ambreen from outside her bedroom door, that after years of introspection he had realised his sins and wanted to make amends and had married her. He asked for her forgiveness and promised that he will protect her honour and never ever make her unhappy. Eventually Ambreen relented and opened the door to Elias. Elias again apologised to Ambreen and told her that he would turn over a new leaf and would never remind her of that horrific incident. Ambreen accompanied Elias back to his house.

Sohail and Samina were delighted and felt relieved to see that Elias had come out of his obsession of washing hands frequently. He, though, remained religious and always thanked God for giving him such happiness. Since Elias and Ambreen were now blissfully settled in their married life, Sohail, Samina, Imtiaz and Fatima started preparing for the wedding of Akmal and Sakina.

There is a higher court
Than courts of justice
And that is
The court of conscience.
It supersedes
All other courts

Mahatma Gandhi

Shattered Dreams

It was not the usual Monday morning for Detective Inspector Peter Callan at Scotland Yard. He had three strange deaths on his file to resolve. He was asked by his boss Chief Inspector David Smith to investigate the deaths of three professional people who had died in a forest in Litchfield in Hertfordshire which is a designated area for pheasant hunting. They all had licensed shotguns and had managed to shoot down two pheasants. There was no apparent cause of their deaths. Peter Callan was the most successful detective who had solved many murder mysteries.

Apparently there seemed to be no connection, except that all three were very close friends and of a similar age. One was a naval commander in Pakistan. The second was a kidney specialist in Los Angeles and the third a medical practitioner in London.

The Detective Inspector was bemused. He found diaries left by each person and going through them, he found similarities, connections and all the missing pieces of the jigsaw of these bizarre deaths.

He was so fascinated by the stories and descriptions in the diaries that he compiled his own report in a dramatic fashion combining all the three diaries. It laid bare a mind boggling story.

The three protagonists were Munir, Iqbal and Anil. They all came from modest backgrounds. They struggled through school days.

They hardly received much pocket money. Their parents could barely afford their school fees let alone the pocket money.

They cleared their GCSE exams and joined the college. Munir Ahmed was very patriotic and wanted to join the navy and serve his country. Ansar Iqbal and Anil Dhawan wanted to join the medical college. They all had their dreams. Munir wanted to achieve the highest post in the navy, that of an Admiral. Iqbal wanted to marry the girl of his choice, his so called dream girl and aspired to be known to the world as a perfect couple. While Anil wanted to be an Orthopaedic surgeon.

Munir applied for naval Cadet College in Petaro, which was the second cadet college after Hasan Abdal, to be established initially at Mirpurkhas in 1957 and shifted to its present location in 1959. Cadet College Petaro is a residential institution, established at Petaro on a campus of 700 acres. It is located 30 kilometers from Hyderabad on the Indus highway. Munir wasn't particularly a brilliant student but very hard working and managed to get admission to the Cadet College.

Anil was a year senior to Iqbal. He was not a bright student either but also very hard working with a sincere desire to get admission in the medical college. Iqbal, unlike the other two, was a brilliant student. He never had to slog hard for his exams, as he had a tremendous grasping power and could learn most of his study subjects by reading once only. Both Anil and Iqbal managed to gain admission at Liaquat Medical College Jamshoro, the former by virtue of his hard work and the latter through his sheer brilliance.

Liaquat Medical College Jamshoro in the Sindh province is located on the right bank of river Indus. It is 16 kilometers away from the historical city of Hyderabad and only 14 kilometers away from Cadet College Petaro. Liaquat Medical College Jamshoro was also a residential institution like Petaro.

As Petaro and Jamshoro are close by, all three friends would meet whenever convenient on weekends and during their holidays. They would often talk about their dreams, not forgetting how hard they had to work to clear all their exams.

Munir made another friend at Petaro called Sadiq, who came from Karachi. Karachi is a wonderful historical city and was once the capital of Pakistan. Now the capital of Pakistan is Islamabad and Karachi has become the capital of Sindh province.

Karachi is the largest city, main seaport and financial centre of Pakistan. The city has an estimated population of twenty million. Karachi is the most populous city in the country and the third largest in terms of population in the world. It is Pakistan's centre of banking, industry and economic activity. The city is a hub of higher education in south Asia and the Muslim world. Karachi is the location of the port of Karachi and port Bin Qasim, the two busiest and largest ports of the country. After the independence of Pakistan, population of Karachi soared dramatically when hundreds of thousands of muhajirs from India and other parts of south Asia came to settle in there.

The city is located in the south of the country, along the coastline meeting the Arabian Sea. It is locally known as "City of Lights" and "The Bride of Cities" for its liveliness and "The City of Quaid" having been the birth and burial place of Quaid-e-Azam, the founder of Pakistan, Muhammed Ali Jinah, who made the city his home after Pakistan's independence from the British Raj on 14th August 1947.

Munir used to visit Karachi frequently. He knew that his practical naval training will be at Karachi so he was keen to see and get to know the city well. His friend Sadiq was happy for Munir to visit Karachi and stay with him at his parents's house during the holidays. Sadiq's father Salim Khan was also a retired naval officer. Salim Khan, impressed by his son's friend Munir's manners, honesty and forthright demeanour came to grow fond of him. Munir also respected Salim Khan like his own father.

Sadiq had a sister called Jabeen. Inevitably Munir came in contact with Jabeen whenever he stayed at Sadiq's house. Soon Munir found himself falling in love with Jabeen. Jabeen was somewhat shy in the beginning but she too fell in love with Munir. It did not escape Salim Khan's notice to see that his daughter liked Munir and sensed that Munir too had the same feelings towards her.

Meanwhile Iqbal was on the lookout for his dream girl. He had a crush on a pretty girl called Noreen in his class when he was a teenager but Noreen showed no interest in him. He tried to be friendly with her but she was unresponsive to his advances. He kept stalking her and would try sitting next to her in the class. This annoyed Noreen no end and one day she sent her mother to Iqbal's house to request his parents to ask Iqbal to refrain from pestering her daughter. Iqbal's parents were embarrassed and warned Iqbal that if he did not stop bothering Noreen, he will be removed from that school. This put paid to the first one sided crush which Iqbal had not even been able to advance yet.

However this did not deter Iqbal from admiring pretty girls. His eyes were always on the lookout for attractive girls. In the medical college he was captivated by a beautiful girl named Shaheen. Shaheen was also quite impressed with Iqbal. Iqbal was undoubtedly a talented boy. He had a good grasping power. He could remember his lectures and medical work without revising the second time. He was one of the favourite students of most of the professors in the medical college. Shaheen used to seek Iqbal's help in her studies. Iqbal was of course more than ready to help and this way he was able to be in close proximity of Shaheen and get to know her better. He was also a very good speaker and often used to win various debating competitions in college. He was much admired and looked up to by most of the fair sex in his college.

Anil had similar feelings for fair sex as any young man would but felt hampered by being a Hindu in a predominantly Muslim country. He was also a very different individual from Iqbal. He was generally an introvert and a quiet person. He was very hard working though not as brilliant like Iqbal. He also became a good orator like Iqbal. This had created more bonding between the two because they regularly participated in debating competitions, always vying to win the trophy for the best speaker.

Anil secretly admired a Muslim girl called Khurshid but was well aware of the hindrances in his way to taking his friendship any further. He found himself at a major disadvantage because he was born a Hindu. Perhaps frequent snide remarks and whispered comments whenever he passed a group of fellow students, not in his immediate circle of friends, led him to believe he was not one of them. His love for a Muslim girl would have led to bloodshed and possible unrest in the college. He had to be content with just admiring Khurshid's beauty from afar without daring to express it openly.

Munir, Iqbal and Anil had always had their disparate dreams to achieve their goals. They all worked very hard so that they would pass their exams and get the basic degree.

Munir was the first to clear his engineering degree from the naval college. Iqbal and Anil both congratulated him on his success. He joined the naval ship at Karachi as an engineer for practical training.

Iqbal's love affair meanwhile came to an abrupt end when Shaheen's parents arranged to get her married to someone else. Being an Asian girl she did not protest and gave in to her parent's wishes. Shaheen got married to a rich businessman. This broke Iqbal's heart and he went into depression.

It was Munir and Anil who pulled Iqbal out of his depression. No sooner had he recovered from depression, he managed to have yet another affair. This time it was with the most beautiful girl in the whole medical college. Her name was Mahtab, which literally means moonshine. She used to shine like the moon in the whole college. Naturally there were plenty of boys who craved after her companionship. Mahtab was a smart and streetwise girl. She knew that she was beautiful and used that to her full advantage. She was very choosy. She saw to it that she made very few friends. Iqbal was one of them. He did his best to attract her by writing poetic verses and showering her with gifts. Their affair became the hottest story of college. They would often meet after college in restaurants and went to movies together. This went on for two years. Still Mahtab kept Iqbal at an arm's length. In the end during the final year of medicine she married a professor in their college. This really was the last straw for poor Iqbal. He decided to leave Pakistan after he finished his degree to find the girl of his dreams in some foreign land.

Anil was the second among his friends to clear his medical degree MBBS (Bachelor of medicine and Bachelor of surgery). Apparently he too was not happy to continue living in Pakistan. He had witnessed the war in 1965 between Pakistan and India. He knew of the hatred that prevailed against Hindus in Pakistan. But he still had to do a one year house job to qualify for registration to work abroad. He still had his dream of becoming an Orthopaedic surgeon for which he needed proper training. He did his best to learn as much as he could in Pakistan but the conditions there were not conducive to getting a good training. The consultants were preoccupied with their private practice rather than teaching or mentoring their junior staff. He did acquire some kissing experiences with the nurses though, during his house job but he did not want to get involved any more than that with those nurses who were mainly Christians. He appeared for ECFMG examination required for US and failed but he did manage to get a job voucher for England.

Iqbal was the last of the three friends to clear his medical degree a year after Anil. During his medical college years he was the most popular student. He was a good debater, good writer and a good poet. He was editor of the Urdu magazine in the college and wrote quite a few stories and poetries, which were highly appreciated in college. He did his house job in Seventh Day Hospital in Karachi. He had always been a brilliant student and now a good doctor and wanted to get higher education. He passed his ECFMG examination and left for America. There he applied for job in Wayne University in Detroit and was appointed as Chief Resident in the University College.

Munir was the first among the three friends to get married. He was very much in love with Jabeen. Once he secured his degree from Petaro, Jabeen's father was quite happy for them to get married. Munir was married to Jabeen in a simple ceremony at Karachi. Sadly both Iqbal and Anil could not attend his marriage but they sent congratulatory telegrams to him. After marriage he became more focused on his dream to reach to the top post of naval Admiral. By dint of his hard work and dedication he soon achieved the rank of Lieutenant Commodore in Pakistan Navy.

Anil left for London as soon as he had completed the pre-requirements for registration to work overseas. He was very focused on becoming a consultant in Orthopedics. London is the capital city of England and the United Kingdom. Located on the River Thames, London has been a major settlement for two millennia, its history going back to its founding by the Romans, who named it Londinium. The bulk of this conurbation forms the London region and the Greater London governed by the elected Mayor of London. London contains World Heritage Sites The Tower of London, Kew Gardens, Westminster Abbey, Buckingham Palace, The London Eye, Piccadilly Circus, St Paul's Cathedral, Tower Bridge and Trafalgar Square to name a few.

Anil had come from Pakistan which is a tropical country and felt too cold in June when he reached London. He found it quite difficult to settle in the beginning as he had no friends or any relations in London. Eventually he came across one of his friends from his college, who helped him to get registered with General Medical Council and the Medical Protection Society so that he could apply for a job. His first job was in casualty department at St Lennard's Hospital in east London.

Iqbal was finding his feet in Detroit city. Detroit is the largest city in the US state of Michigan, and is the seat of Wayne County. It is the major city among the primarily cultural, financial and transportation centres in the Metro Detroit area, a region of 5.2 million people. Detroit is known for being home to the main American automobile industry and is aptly dubbed the Motor City.

Iqbal was still looking for his dream girl in America. He had plenty of flings, being a romantic by nature. Most of them were just one-night stands. He was getting frustrated, till one day when he hit the bullseye. He met Jenny, an American girl, who seemed to fit in with his dreams. She was the girl he had been waiting for. She was the most beautiful girl in the world for him. Soon they started living together. Jenny too was absolutely besotted with him and was always able to anticipate what he wanted. She would get his briefcase and handkerchief ready for him when he left for his college just like an Asian wife would. She loved all his habits good and bad. Iqbal was getting thoroughly spoiled by Jenny. He told Munir and Anil about Jenny, and they both encouraged Iqbal to marry her. Iqbal was in two minds. He was not sure how Jenny will fit in with Pakistani culture but he promised to his friends that he will give it a serious thought.

Meanwhile in Pakistan Munir was blessed with a beautiful daughter who they named Nadia. Munir and Jabeen were over the moon. They doted on Nadia and enjoyed watching her growing up. They watched her smiling, crawling, standing and eventually running. It is such a joy to see your own child reaching milestones. The birth of Nadia brought a promotion for Munir. He was appointed as Commodore. This was one more step towards his dream of becoming an Admiral in Navy.

Anil gradually started to feel at home in London. He eventually managed to get a job in Orthopaedics at St Lennard's hospital for eighteen months. This gave him a springboard to achieve his dream to become an Orthpaedic surgeon. He applied for a study leave to prepare for FRCS (Fellow of Royal College of Surgeons). FRCS is in two parts. He also applied for the special course to attend for preparing for FRCS. His hospital and the consultant Mr Wordsworth were very helpful and arranged to pay for his FRCS course.

Anil studied hard for his FRCS course. The course was of twelve weeks duration and Anil was required to attend daily at the Royal College. It was proving quite hard and he would get exhausted by the end of the day. He also had to revise the subjects during

86

weekends, besides needing to relax during the weekends to recharge his batteries for the rigourous five days a week course. He craved female company for his relaxation. After all he was a virile young man with normal sexual desires. He managed to find a Malaysian girl with whom he was able to relax and fulfill his sexual urges.

On the other side of the Atlantic, Iqbal was finding it hard making up his mind about Jenny. He always had in his mind to marry a Pakistani girl in America, even though Jenny had everything he wanted in a wife and she was indeed the girl of his dreams. For the time being though he put his mind to getting fellowship in Nephrology (kidney physician). Being a brilliant student he soon achieved his fellowship from University of Chicago and American College of Physicians. He was appointed an assistant professor in Nephrology in University of Chicago and Illinois. Chicago is a city in the US state of Illinois, and is the third most populous city in the United States, and the most populous city in the American Midwest with a population over 2.8 million. The city is an international hub for finance, commerce, industry, telecommunications, and transportations, with O'hare International Airport being the second busiest airport in the world in terms of traffic movements.

Around this time Commodore Munir was posted for few months at Plymouth in South West England for further training. This was a very good opportunity for the three friends to meet and get together again. London being about half way between Pakistan and America, they agreed to rendezvous there. Iqbal took a week off his work and came to London. That week turned out to be the best for the three friends. They saw all the main places of interest in London. They took a bus pass every day and saw practically the whole of London. Among those was the famous Madame Tussaud's Museum. Marie Tussaud was born in 1761 in Strasbourg, France. Her mother worked as a housekeeper for Dr. Philippe Curtius in Bern, Switzerland, who was a physician skilled in wax modelling. Curtius taught Tussaud the art of wax modelling. Tussaud created her first wax figure, of Voltaire in the year 1777. Other famous people at that time include Jean-Jacques Rousseau and Benjamin Franklin. During the French

Revolution she created face masks using the executed citizens.

After the death of Dr. Philipe Curtius, Marie Tussaud inherited his vast collection of wax models and spent the next thirty three years travelling around Europe. As a result of Napoleonic wars, she was unable to return to France. By 1835 Marie had settled down in Baker Street, London, and opened a museum. Now there are more Madame Tussaud Museums in America, Europe, Asia and Australia.

Munir was happy to tell his friends that he was well on his way to becoming Admiral. Anil was happy to report that he was working hard for FRCS to achieve his dream of becoming Orthopaedic surgeon but Iqbal mentioned that though he had met his dream girl, an American, he was still not sure whether he would marry her because all along he had wanted to marry a Pakistani girl. Both friends tried to persuade Iqbal to marry Jenny but he was not altogether sure. Iqbal went back to US after one week but Munir still had few more months of training to do at Plymouth, so he met Anil frequently in London.

During this time Anil mentioned to Munir that he led an isolated life in London and felt lonely. He no longer wished to carry on with the girls just for sexual gratification. He wanted to marry and settle down in life. Munir suggested he wrote to his parents to find a suitable girl for him. Anil took his advice. The parents did find a girl and Anil accepted the proposal without seeing the girl because he was very obedient to his parents. But when he went to Pakistan for marriage, his parents had some argument with girl's parents and the marriage never took place. He came back to London downhearted, very depressed and felt lonely again.

Anil had an elder brother in India who he looked up to the most after his father. As there is large Hindu community in India, he wrote to his brother in India at his father's suggestion to find a suitable match for him. He also gave his word of honour to his brother that he will marry the girl whoever his brother would choose for him.

Meanwhile Commodore Munir had gone back to Pakistan after

completing his training at Plymouth. He was again blessed with his second daughter whom they named Shahla. This coincided with his promotion to Rear Admiral. Munir was very pleased as he was getting closer to his goal of becoming Admiral. The births of his children had proved lucky for him in gaining promotions.

However for Anil things were not going well. He failed in his FRCS. He was already lonely and depressed and had no stamina left to study any more. He could not get his mind together for a second attempt at FRCS. He also had to put up with discouraging banter by his colleagues at the FRCS course that he may not achieve his fellowship even after repeated attempts. His dream of becoming an Orthopaedic surgeon seemed too distant now and beyond his reach. He took an easy option to change the line and go for a degree in Anaesthetics instead. He believed that it was easier to achieve diploma in Anaesthetics than FRCS in Orthopaedics. He was well trained in Anaesthetics at St Margaret Hospital, Epping in Essex county of Greater London. But he was restless. He wanted to achieve diploma in Anaesthetics quickly so that he could go for FRCS in Anaesthetics. Unfortunately this too proved a bridge too far. He failed because of his impetuosity. As it was he found Anaesthetics very non clinical and did not enjoy the year in Anaesthetics. He decided to change the line yet again, this time to General Practice, the so called Jack of all, master of none. He managed to get a vocational training job in General Practice where he had to do two years in hospital and one year as a trainee in General Practice under a GP.

Iqbal on the other hand was on a different crossroads. He very much loved his American girlfriend Jenny. They both were in love and devoted to each other. Iqbal however had always wanted to marry a Pakistani girl and settle down in Pakistan. As he was very much in love with Jenny, he did ask her to marry him and go with him to Pakistan. Jenny though eager to marry him was not too keen to move to Pakistan. This virtually ended their love affair which Iqbal always regretted throughout his life.

Meanwhile Munir had his third child, a boy named Ali. Not

unexpectedly this too coincided with his further promotion to Vice Admiral, bringing him to just one step away from his dream of becoming an Admiral. Munir was very happy with his progress in the navy and of course he was congratulated by both Anil and Iqbal. They were both pleased for Munir that he was so close to achieving his goal.

Anil was still very lonely. His parents wrote and kept encouraging him to wait patiently for his brother in India to find a suitable girl for his marriage. His elder brother had promised that he would do his best to find a suitable match for him. But Anil was so frustrated that he started going out with any willing girl, though he was not prepared to settle down with any of them. He enjoyed the female company as a man but did not fall in love with any of them. He wanted to marry the girl who would make a home for him and be an ideal housewife and look after him.

God was in his Heaven and all was well with the world. Lady Luck suddenly smiled at Anil. He was introduced to a ravishing Indian beauty by a friend in London. She was a doctor by profession and very beautiful. He consulted Munir and Iqbal for their advice. They both were very supportive and advised him to go ahead. He contacted his parents in Pakistan and asked for their permission and blessings. He got engaged to Radha with his own, as well as her parents consent who were in London at that time.

But then came an unexpected surprise in a letter from Anil's brother in India that he had found a very suitable girl for him to get married. He had also enclosed a photograph of the girl in which she looked attractive. He felt morally obliged to accept the girl his brother had proposed for him at his own behest. He considered his brother like his father and wanted to give up his chosen girl Radha. On the other hand he had given Radha's parents his word of honour that he would marry their daughter. He was in a quandary. He faced a dilemma. It was like choosing between devil and the deep Sea. At this juncture his fiancée came to his rescue.

Radha helped him come out of his predicament. She told him,

"You cannot let your brother or anyone else take decisions about your life, you are an adult and should make your own choices regarding your life partner. How could you marry a girl you have not even met." He felt very frustrated but took a firm decision to marry Radha. Anil wrote to his brother that he was going ahead with his decision to marry Radha. By doing so he burnt his boat regarding his relations with his brother. His brother never forgave him for that and wrote him a final letter breaking all relations with him for life. Munir and Iqbal sent him congratulations when he finally married Radha.

Iqbal was also heartbroken after the breakup of his relationship with Jenny. He now felt very lonely and desperately wanted to get married. He wrote to his parents that he was willing to marry any girl of their choice. He was so desperate that he did not want even to see the girl before marriage. His mother was very happy to get this letter from Iqbal. Salma was chosen by his mother and sister and Iqbal got married to Salma in a simple ceremony at Karachi. Munir and Anil could not attend his marriage at such a short notice but sent their best wishes.

Now all three friends were finally married. Munir was Vice Admiral in Pakistan Navy. Iqbal was a successful kidney physician and Anil was a partner in General Practice of three doctors in London.

Iqbal had in mind to earn quick money and go back to Pakistan. He was invited to establish a kidney unit at Shah Saudi University in Saudi Arabia with a lucrative pay package. He took that post to make a quick buck for establishing his own kidney unit in Pakistan.

Saudi Arabia officially known as the Kingdom of Saudi Arabia, is the largest Arab state in western Asia by land area (870000 sq miles), constituting the bulk of Arabia Peninsula and the second-largest in the Arab world after Algeria. Its population is estimated to consist of 16 million natives and an additional 9 million registered foreign expatriates and 2 million illegal immigrants.

The Kingdom of Saudi Arabia was founded by Ibn Saud in 1932. The Saudi Arabian Government has been an absolute monarchy since its inception and describes itself as being Islamic. Saudi Arabia is the birthplace of Islam and the Kingdom is sometimes called 'the Land of Two Holy Mosques' in reference to Al-Masjid al-Haram in Mecca and Al-Masjid al-Nawabi in Medina, the two holiest places in Islam.

Saudi Arabia has the world's second largest oil reserves which are largely concentrated around Eastern Province. Oil accounts for more than 95% of exports and 70% government revenue, although the share of non-oil economy has been growing recently. This has facilitated the transformation of an underdeveloped desert kingdom into one of the world's wealthiest nations. Vast oil reserves have prompted rapid modernisation, such as the creation of a welfare state. It also has the world's sixth largest natural gas reserves. It is the only country in the world where women are not allowed to drive.

After establishing the kidney unit in Saudi Arabia Iqbal went back to Pakistan to work in Agha Khan University Karachi to establish kidney unit. After four years, he went back to Faisal University in Saudi Arabia to work as a visiting professor at their invitation.

The lives of the friends were going smoothly and blissfully at long last but destiny had other ideas. Personal tragedies struck all three friends. Vice Admiral Munir was accused of taking bribe for recommending an unsafe naval ship which should have been damage resistant and armed with weapon systems. Munir was the chief engineer responsible for checking and examining all the combat warships before they were purchased by Pakistan Navy. He was found guilty of recommending a combat ship which was not worthy of Pakistan Navy. He was remanded in custody pending an appeal in the Supreme Court. Anil and Iqbal could not believe this. Munir was the most honest person who would not be bribed even in his wildest dreams. They both sent their deepest sympathies to him and his family and prayed for his acquittal in the Supreme Court on appeal.

Anil was still in his third year of training for General Practice. He was hungry for making quick money whenever he got a chance. He had a fair amount of free time on his hands during training. He started working as a relief doctor in neighbouring GP surgeries. It boosted his income which he thought would come in handy when he and Radha decided to buy their house. In one of the social meetings he met one Dr Sharma who used to arrange relief doctors for hospitals. When Dr Sharma came to know that Anil had experience in Anaestheics, he suggested that Anil should work as a relief doctor in hospital as an Anesthetist because it paid well. Anil was happy and agreed that he would work when he is free on any weekend.

Dr Sharma phoned Anil a few days later and offered him a relief Anaesthetic job in Orpington Hospital Surrey for a weekend when he was free. The money was good for a weekend's work and Anil jumped at the opportunity. Unfortunately during a routine Anaesthetic for an appendix operation something went wrong. A child had come for an operation and due to lack of oxygen the child went into coma.The hospital authorities and child's parents were very unhappy and indignant. Anil was accused of manslaughter and was released on bail in the Coroner's court. Radha was very upset at hearing this serious charge against her husband in the very first few weeks of their marriage but she and the Medical Protection Society solicitor assured Anil that they will fight his case in the criminal court at Old Bailey.

The Central Criminal Court of England and Wales, commonly known as the Old Bailey after the street on which it stands, is a court in London and one of a number of buildings housing the Crown Court. The Crown Court sitting at the Central Criminal Court deals with major criminal cases from Greater London and in exceptional cases, from other parts of England and Wales. Part of the present building stands on the site of the medieval Newgate gaol, on Old Bailey, a road which follows the line of the City of London's fortified wall (or bailey), which runs from Ludgate Hill to the junction of Newgate Street and Holborn Viaduct. The present building was officially opened in 1907. It was designed by E. W. Mountford. Above the main entrance the inscription says "Defend the children of poor & punish the wrongdoer." King Edward VII opened the courthouse. Trials at the Old Bailey are open to public subject to stringent security procedures.

While in Saudi Arabia, a tragedy had befallen Iqbal. His wife Salma gave birth to a baby boy. Unfortunately he was born with 'Cleft palate and Hare lip', a birth defect with fissure in the upper lip and palate. He and Salma were obviously very distraught. Iqbal decided to go back to US for medical treatment of his son Usman. He had more cofidence in American doctors who were obviously more advanced in treating these conditions. It took two years and quite a few operations and plastic surgery to rectify the defect. It was more than 95% successful.

Iqbal was reasonably pleased with the result. He had now decided to stay back in America. He had by now lost his burning desire to go back to Pakistan. He became a partner in a practice as a kidney specialist and medical director for Dialysis unit around Los Angeles. He built a sumptuous house for his family in Alta Loma in California. Shortly after, he and Salma had their second child. This time they were blessed with a lovely daughter whom they named Mahrukh. She was very pretty and filled Iqbal's heart with joy. He thanked God for giving him a healthy child. Of course Munir and Anil did not forget to send their congratulations despite their own difficult personal situations at that time.

The tragedy struck Iqbal again, this time with a vengeance. His son Usman developed Lymphoma. Lymphoma is a type of blood cancer that occurs when B or T lymphocytes, the white cells that form part of immune system and help protect the body from infection and disease, begin behaving abnormally. Lymphoma may develop in many parts of body including the lymph nodes, spleen, bone marrow, blood or other organs and eventually they form a mass of cells called a tumour. In Usman's case it presented a solid mass of lymphoid cells around neck area.

Iqbal consulted a top specialist in Lymphoma in California. He advised chemotherapy, radiotherapy followed by bone marrow transplant. As it had been diagnosed very quickly and treatment started straight away and lymphoma was not very malignant it did not spread to other parts of body. It took nearly two years to completely eradicate the lymphoma from Usman's body. Iqbal thanked God for giving Usman a new lease of life. Iqbal became very spiritual after this episode in his life. He went and performed the Haj in Mecca to thank God for his mercy. These two horrendous episodes in his son Usman's life were very traumatic and agonizing for him.

Meanwhile Vice Admiral Munir was released on bail pending an appeal. He was stripped of his rank of Vice Admiral. As law and courts take time, Munir had to wait for more than two years before his case came up for hearing in the Supreme Court. Munir had always been a very honourable and ethical person throughout his life. He never had made illicit money. As the fees for Supreme Court barrister are very high, he had to dip into all his savings to pay for them. He even had to sell his wife's jewellery to fight the case. His barrister was a very competent and a thorough professional. It took more than one year in the court to fight his case. The public prosecutor was an able lawyer but the defence lawyer fought tooth and nail for Munir.

Eventually it transpired that the ship in question had indeed been rejected by Munir but overruled by his boss who had accepted a hefty backhander and forged Munir's signature. Munir had refused to accept any money and was not a party to the deal which his boss had agreed. Munir had been basically framed by his boss and had been sent to jail without any wrongdoing on his part.

Munir was honourably exonerated and cleared of all corruption charges with no blot on his integrity and was reinstated to the post of Vice Admiral. He and his family were relieved of the constant mental strain they had endured for three years. He was congratulated by Anil and Iqbal.

In London Anil was going through his stress of verdict of manslaughter. It was like the fabled sword of Damocles hanging over his head. It is a Greek fable when Damocles told the king Dionysius that how fortunate a king can be that he can dictate his power to his subjects. Dionysius asked Damocles to become the king for a day and see what a king has to deal with. All was going well with Damocles till he saw a sharp sword hovering over his head suspended from the ceiling by a single horse hair. Damocles then realised the responsibilities of a king and gave up his desire to become king.

Anil had now finished his three year training for general practice. He was desperate to get a job in General Practice. He applied all over UK to find a job but was unsuccessful repeatedly because he had to tell at the interviews that he had a court case pending an appeal against verdict of manslaughter. Nobody was willing to give him a job when his future was uncertain. He even travelled up to Scotland for an interview where he was selected but when he informed them about his pending court case of manslaughter, the employing doctor did not want to take any risks in employing him.

Anil was getting very depressed. But God was looking after him. He applied for an interview just outside London. It was a partnership of three doctors. One of the partners was retiring. He was interviewed by the remaining two partners, one Englishman and the other an Indian. The Indian doctor was not keen on employing him, but the English doctor, being the senior partner was impressed by Anil's credentials and his honesty in disclosing that he had a court case pending against him.

Anil was employed as a salaried partner for the first year. The Indian partner was not too happy but gave in due to pressure from the senior English partner but made sure that Anil was given the minimum salary. Throughout these few months, Anil's wife Radha who had started work in gynaecology department at a local hospital, provided stout support to him. Anil was very happy to have at least landed a job and did not quibble about his salary.

God was now performing magic for Anil. Anil was happy with his job and the only worry that made him lose sleep at night was the court case of manslaughter hanging over his head. Out of blue one day at the surgery, the solicitor from Medical Protection Society phoned to inform him that the Director of Public Prosecution was dropping the case against him. Anil could not believe his ears. He had to ask again to make sure that he had heard it correctly. Once he was sure, he gave this good news to his wife and his senior partner. Both were very pleased for him.

The solicitor from Medical Protection Society had explained to Anil that he had to appear at Old Bailey criminal court as a formality and plead 'Not Guilty'. A few days later Anil appeared at the Old Bailey. He was made to stand in the dock and pleaded 'Not Guilty'. Anil's wife was also present in the court. Anil and Radha were relieved from the stress they had undergone for over a year. The Queen's Council told Anil to tell his grandchildren that, "He has been to the Old Bailey." Anil duly received congratulations from Munir and Iqbal following his acquittal from the verdict of manslaughter.

EPILOGUE

Now all three friends had retired. They decided to meet and reflect on "What they had achieved and what they had lost in life."

They agreed to meet in London as it is more or less midway between Pakistan and the US. Munir came over from Pakistan and Iqbal from the US. They thought that fresh country air in the forest will do them good and they will go for pheasant shooting in Litchfield area in Hertfordshire. The three friends were happy listening to each other's tales.

Munir recounted his story of fame and power. He was very happily settled with his attractive wife Jabeen and two daughters and a son. His daughter Nadia had become a solicitor and she did get married but unfortunately her marriage did not last long. She was divorced within a year which upset the whole family and Nadia was now back home living with them. Nadia was a brilliant lawyer but with her delicate frame and diminutive stature people always wondered how she fought the cases in court, and her clients were amazed at the way she presented her legal arguments when trying to defend them. She had 90% success rate with her cases.

Munir's other daughter Shahla became a banker and worked for a major bank in London. She did Master's degree in banking in London. Shahla was a clever girl and during her days at the college she fell in love with a boy from India, who was doing PhD at the same college. The only problem Shahla faced in marrying her boyfriend Joseph was that his being a Christian might not be agreeable to her Muslim parents. This is where Anil and Radha proved to be of great help. Shahla requested Radha and Anil to meet Joseph. They found that Joseph was one of the nicest persons they had ever met. He was very polite and considerate and came from a cultured family. Shahla requested Anil to convince her father that he was the right boy for her. Munir agreed to get Shahla married to Joseph provided he accepted the Islamic faith. Joseph agreed to that condition and got converted to Islam by a Muslim priest. He and Shahla were married with the blessings of Munir and Jabeen.

Munir's third child Ali followed in his father's footsteps and joined the Pakistan Navy. Ali was still a bachelor. He wanted to enjoy life before he gave up freedom of a bachelor. Munir acknowledged that he had his fair share of happiness in life but for his first daughter Nadia's divorce which had upset him immensely. The false accusation of being dishonest and accepting bribe was a huge blow to his moral values, Munir added ruefully. His few months in jail were the worst days of his life. His only regret in life was that he could not reach the highest position of Admiral in navy and his dream remained unfulfilled. Yet he had one consolation that his son Ali might complete his dream and some day in future become an Admiral.

Anil narrated his story next. He said he was very lucky in many ways. His wife Radha was very beautiful. Interrupting Anil, Iqbal commented if she had been a Muslim, she would have been his dream girl. Anil went on to tell more about Radha's talents. Her figure was perfect, with lips like petals of pink rose and eyes shining like blue diamonds. She was a master cook and very good in sewing and making dresses. She had all the qualities of a good wife. She had rather expensive taste. Her best friends were diamonds. Well in a way you can say 'Diamond girl deserves Diamonds'

Anil made sure he gave Radha diamonds on her birthdays. But she liked jewellery so much that she bought diamond and gold whenever she wanted and Anil never objected because he wanted to see her happy. Anil also mentioned that God had been kind to him and had blessed him with two lovely boys. The elder son was very bright. He did Economics degree from Cambridge and MBA from New York. He had married an Australian girl and was blessed with an adorable daughter Simran and lovely son Roshan. His elder son was well settled in US.

Anil's younger son Samir had become a medical practitioner and had taken over the practice from his parents, who both had retired from General Practice. Samir was a computer wizard and had transformed the practice and had modernised with so many new things that his was considered the best practice in the area. Samir was still a bachelor because he was very choosy. He had seen many girls. He went out with few of them for a coffee and sometimes for dinner with some of them but most of time he found they were not his type and were on different wavelengths from him. But Anil added that now he had liked a girl from New York and there was a good chance that he would marry soon and settle down. Samir preferred a destination wedding because he met a girl away from home. Anil and Radha were happy for him and had given him full freedom to choose his wedding venue.

Anil was still upset about his tragic episode during Anaestheic work and the stress he went through with the agony of verdict of the manslaughter over his head. He also felt very bitter that he could not achieve his dream of becoming an Orthopaedic surgeon. He blamed it on his poor training and lack of motivation. But it was now a bridge too far. He may have to be reborn to achieve his dream.

Iqbal had a different story to tell. He had become a famous kidney specialist and patients regarded him as a God. Patients came to him in miserable state and he made them live happily for many years. But his marriage was a total failure. His wife despised him because he had a reputation of several love affairs. He was like a stranger in his own house. Salma, his wife used to go to Pakistan whenever she wished. In short his marriage was on the rocks. Iqbal regretted that he let go of Jenny, his dream girl, due to his own stubbornness.

He was however happy that God had given him a dutiful son Usman, even though he went through a lot of trials and tribulations during his Hare lip and Lymphoma phases. But with God's grace Usman was now a very healthy young man and about to complete his law degree. He was also happy with his lovely daughter Mahrukh who was aspiring to be a dentist. Iqbal admitted that he was very sad that he did not get his dream girl.

The diaries ended there. Peter Callan told his boss that coroner was unable to determine the exact cause of their deaths. The only clue he found was that a lightening had struck in the forest and their camping tent was destroyed.

The weird thing was that all three friends had died exactly at the same time because their hearts had stopped at the same time. He came to the conclusion that all three friends were 'SOUL MATES'. True friendship is an identity of souls rarely to be found in this world and they died because of their shattered dreams!

Friendship to be real must ever sustain
the weight of honest differences,
However sharp they may be
The test of friendship is assistance in adversity,
And that too,
Unconditional assistance

Mahatma Gandhi

Crown Of Thorns

Dr Munir Ahmed was watching the live coverage of a rally in India, on the American television network CNN. The new Prime Minister of India, Kumar Trivedi was to make an important announcement in regard to the steps he contemplated for ensuring peace with Pakistan. Munir had known Kumar since childhood in Pakistan and was proud that Kumar had valued his friendship over the years even after his migration to India. He had keenly watched Kumar's political rise and finally his ascension to the highest office in the Government of India.

At the same time Professor William Smith was watching this historic event live on BBC at his home in London with swelling pride. Smith had known Kumar for many years since his student days at King's College in London not only as his favourite student, but also having been his mentor and guide. He had largely groomed Kumar, who always regarded his views and opinions on issues relating to India and Pakistan with utmost respect.

Kumar had hardly commenced his speech, when gunshots erupted and hit the Prime Minister, who slumped on the stage. There was total pandemonium with people running around pell-mell. The security ring was immediately tightened and all who attended were thoroughly frisked manually as well as with metal detectors before being allowed to leave. Though, no weapons were found on anybody, some persons were rounded up and detained under suspicion. The television channels interrupted their live telecasts to inform the

101

viewers that the Indian Prime Minister had been shot and was grievously injured and had been taken to the All India Institute of Medical Sciences (AIIMS). It was not certain how critical he was, and neither the assassin, nor the weapon were found.

The army was called in to maintain security in the capital, as there was a fear of rioting. Large crowds who had taken to the streets and converged around the hospital area were dispersed. Rumours regarding the identity of the assassin were rife and there was a real risk of communal riots breaking out. In the public mind the hand of a foreign power, particularly Pakistan was suspected.

In the intensive care unit at AIIMS, doctors, nurses and paramedics worked at feverish pitch to save their dear Prime Minister who symbolized their desire for eternal peace for the nation through his sincere efforts and devotion to the cause. Lying on his bed, Kumar felt that he was sinking in a thick mist. He summoned all his energies in an effort to force open his eyes but saw nothing but a blur. His entire life quickly flashed through his mind, right from the days of his childhood, the sweet memories of his friends, his association with various people, his resolve to bring peace to the subcontinent and finally the regret that he could not achieve what he had set out to do. Then suddenly the whole world blew apart, as if a dark cloud had swallowed the sun.

Both Munir and Smith took the next available flights to India to be with their friend.

Kumar was born in a small town, Kotri, in Sindh, a province of undivided India on the banks of the river Indus. His father was the headmaster of the local high school and was held in high esteem by the local community. His life as a little boy was spent running through green open fields where mango trees were always in full bloom lending a sweet aroma to the atmosphere. He did his schooling in an imposing red brick building over which his father supervised majestically, instilling strict discipline and the right values of life in his pupils. After school, he would play with his friends and classmates Munir, Ramesh, Shahid and Hussein. There was absolutely no rancour among them in spite of belonging to different religions. This was the happiest time of his life.

India's independence arrived in August 1947. It was divided into two parts, the Islamic state of Pakistan and the secular India. Brothers started killing brothers, the humans were transformed into savages, and the fire of prejudice and hatred replaced the love and harmony of those who had coexisted until then as one large happy family. In his early teens, Kumar's little mind could not comprehend what was going on. Kumar's house was situated in a predominately Muslim neighbourhood. He could sense that something terrible was about to happen when he found his parents whispering frequently, petrified with terror in their eyes. The doors were kept locked at all times and constant prayers for safety became a regular routine. The school was closed and there was no contact with his friends.

One dreaded night, he was awakened by shouts and screams and it looked as if the whole house was shaking. He realised that a mob was trying to break open their door and windows. His mother grabbed him and pushed him behind a large cupboard in the corner and asked him to remain there totally quiet. She ran towards the small home temple where his father looking pale and helpless, was kneeling in front of the idol of the family deity, invoking divine help.

The next moment the door was broken and dozens of people armed with cleavers and choppers descended upon his parents. Some of them held burning torches in their hands and in the flickering flames he could see and recognise many familiar faces of neighbours whom he used to call uncles. This was the time when hatred and evil emotions fuelled by religious bigotry wiped out all happy relationships. The next moment he saw his parents being butchered mercilessly and hacked into pieces. They then called out his name and started looking for him. His little mind was terrified awaiting his turn to be killed.

Suddenly a commanding voice ordered them to stop. He peeped and saw Munir's father, Shahnawaz enter the room with his brothers and cousins to defend them. They reminded the mobsters that the headmaster was God's good man and they should not harm him or his family. The mob cleared out and Shahnawaz realised with horror that they were too late to save Kumar's parents. They managed to find Kumar huddled behind a cupboard, terror writ large on his little innocent face.

Shahnawaz decided to take him to the safety of his own house. Kumar never forgot that night when he witnessed the cold blooded murder of his parents. His mind carried the scars of that memory for the rest of his life in spite of the tender and loving care provided to him by Munir's parents.

Although the Pakistan Government had set up a camp for orphaned Hindu children at the district office under army protection, Shahnawaz was still concerned about the deteriorating situation and in particular about Kumar's safety. He decided to shelter him at his house till some relation of Kumar could be located. Three months later, he found Kumar's uncle Lalchand who ran a well-established business in Karachi and had survived the riots. He contacted Lalchand and told him all about little Kumar and how his parents had been the victims of the frenzied mob during the recent riots. Lalchand suggested that under the circumstances Kumar had better continued staying with Shahnawaz for some more time as the situation in Karachi was still tense. Besides, his wife being in hospital recovering from a stomach operation, there would be no one to take care of Kumar in Lalchand's house. While at Shahnawaz's house Munir also kept pleading with his father to let Kumar stay with them as he had grown very fond of him and had come to treat him like his own brother. Kumar continued staying with Shahnawaz.

The school reopened and Kumar and Munir resumed their studies. At this stage, a beautiful girl, Gulnar, a distant cousin of Munir and of their age group, came to stay next door and joined the same school. All three of them would walk to the school and back together. They used to spend as much time as they could in each other's company. Both Munir and Kumar were attracted towards Gulnar. They would often rib each other as to which one of the two would eventually marry Gulnar, who used to laugh at their fantasy.

Lalchand had a flourishing business of supplying sugar throughout western India, which now became part of Pakistan. He used to source his supplies from sugar factories located around Bombay (now known as Mumbai). He had a house in Mumbai and also a trading office there, where he would make frequent visits on business. With the formation of Pakistan, he was doubtful whether he would be permitted to import sugar from India any longer. He therefore started establishing alternative sources of procuring sugar from Ceylon (now known as Sri Lanka) and Kenya. Therefore in spite of the mass exodus of Hindus from Pakistan to India in the wake of partition riots, he decided to stay put in Karachi where he had cultivated close friends in affluent and influential quarters who had indeed saved his life during the riots. He felt he would always be safe among his Muslim friends.

In January 1948, mass looting of Hindu households took place rampantly in Karachi and Lalchand was one of the victims. The jewellery of his wife and all valuable possessions in his house were plundered and he along with his wife had to move into a refugee camp. He thought enough was enough and took the bitter decision to migrate to India. He wound up his business and sold his domestic and business premises at virtually throwaway prices.

Lalchand contacted Shahnawaz and informed him of his decision and requested him to prepare Kumar also for migration. Since Kumar's final examinations were expected to be over by March, they decided to migrate to India in April. Kumar bid a tearful farewell to Munir, his parents and Gulnar and then accompanied by his uncle Lalchand moved to Mumbai in April. They all promised that they would keep in regular touch with each other through letters.

The Government of India had announced that all persons migrating from Pakistan to India by the end of 1948 would be treated as Indian citizens. Immediately after landing in Mumbai they applied for Indian citizenship and duly received citizenship certificates. Since Lalchand already had a house and a trading office in Mumbai, they settled down quickly. Kumar joined a College in Mumbai and Lalchand planned to send him to London for higher education after graduation.

Kumar was very active in his college debating society and was keenly interested in the subjects of political science and history, particularly in India's relationship with Pakistan. Although with the passage of time, the dust of partition, riots and disruption had settled, the sad memories of the brutal killing of his parents still haunted him. He strongly felt that something should be done to remove the deep rooted mutual distrust and hatred between the two countries. His contact with his Pakistani friends Munir and Gulnar was disrupted for lack of communication lines between the two countries and slowly the memories of his childhood began fading away.

Three years later, Lalchand's wife passed away. Kumar had graduated and was ready to leave for London to join the prestigious King's College for a master's degree in political science. Lalchand himself decided to migrate and settle down in USA and start a business activity there.

Kumar stood under the dazzling lights of Piccadilly Circus with mixed feelings. Piccadilly Circus was created in 1819 at the junction with Regent Street, which was being built under the planning of John Nash at the site of a house and garden belonging to a lady Hutton. The circus lost its circular form in 1886 with the construction of Shaftesbury Avenue. The Piccadilly Circus tube station was opened in 1906. In 1928 the station was extensively rebuilt to handle the increase in traffic. Coca-Cola has had a prominent sign at Piccadilly Circus since 1954.

He realised that this was the beginning of the rest of his life and wanted to steer it into proper direction. He had fears and insecurity, also excitement and hope. He summoned up all his spirits and decided to make the most of his new life.

At King's College he met Professor William Smith, who had

spent a long time in British India prior to the partition of the country. He had a deep involvement with Indian politics and was emotionally close to the people of India. Professor Smith was very friendly with Shankar Singh, an upcoming leader of a prominent political party in India called Jai-Hind and had kept a regular contact with him to be abreast of political happenings in that country. At the request of Shankar Singh, the professor agreed to secure admission for his daughter Sheila to King's College as soon as she graduated from Delhi University.

Kumar shared his feelings about the two countries with Professor Smith and his vision of eternal peace between them, where people would live in harmony and reap the benefits of their respective potentials with mutual help. With no close friends at hand, Kumar spent most of his evenings either in the college library studying all the available literature on undivided India in order to understand the undercurrents leading to the partition or with Professor Smith to learn all about the pre-partition situation as personally witnessed by the professor.

One fine morning after almost two years in London, while walking down the steps of the London Museum, somebody tapped on his shoulder from behind and before he could turn around, he was being embraced by somebody with great passion and words: "Oh my God where have you been Kumar? I have been looking for you all over London". It was Munir. Kumar was stunned and lost for words. He was so overcome with emotions that he could hardly speak. He hugged Munir and held him tightly for a few moments. When his emotions settled, he observed through tear-blurred eyes that Gulnar was also standing behind Munir and looking at him with the same old fondness.

They sat in a nearby coffee house catching up on the old happy times. Both Munir and Gulnar told Kumar, how much they had missed him all those years. Munir had completed his MBBS in Pakistan and was in London now to study for the FRCS. He was working at the Hammersmith Hospital and was staying in doctor's quarters provided by the hospital, while Gulnar was pursuing her studies for a Master's degree in Journalism in a nearby college and stayed with an aunt. They had been formally engaged and the wedding would take place in Pakistan as soon as they returned home after completing their studies.

Munir and Gulnar were planning to come back to London after marriage with a view to settling down there. Munir will join the oncology (cancer) department and Gulnar would join as a sub-editor with London Times, a job already offered to her and which she had accepted.

Gulnar had grown up into a pretty young lady with almond eyes, silky long hair and a willowy figure with a majestic bearing. Kumar could hardly take his eyes off her. He indeed envied Munir at his luck for having Gulnar to be his life partner and had the consolation that he would be near them when they returned to London after their marriage. In the meantime, he would enjoy their company for the next two years while they were all studying here. That evening they parted with a promise that they would meet frequently to cement their friendship further.

The three of them met virtually every week over a cup of coffee or an occasional dinner. They would often discuss the situation in the subcontinent. They despaired why there was so much poverty, hatred and suffering across the borders. They always concurred on one point that the common man in both countries wanted no part in the hostilities and it was only the politicians who fuelled and fanned the fanatic fires for their ulterior motives to remain in power. They were open-minded, highly educated, well read and tolerant of each other. They knew that they belonged to different religions, which was the basis for the partition of India but did not think anything of it. Above all they were close friends and enjoyed each other's company. They often wondered why their two countries could not get on with each other like so many other neighbouring countries.

Sometimes the discussions would get heated, but they were always intent on listening to each other's viewpoints. Munir though a Pakistani Muslim was more critical of the Pakistan government than

Kumar was. Likewise, Kumar would often denounce some of the policies pursued by India. They felt that the Kotri with its endless mango plantations, river Indus and plains of Punjab, snowcapped Himalayas of India and fruit orchards of Himachal Pradesh should be enjoyed by all people from both sides of border.

Kumar did not know what Gulnar thought about their religious differences, but he could perceive that while she loved sharing poetry with Munir, she equally enjoyed listening to Kumar's political views and quietly appreciated his feelings. Quite often from Gulnar's remarks and open admiration Kumar suspected that Gulnar was smitten with him. Had he not migrated to India, she might very well have chosen him as her life partner in preference to Munir. The next moment he would dismiss the thought as ridiculous because she was already engaged to his best friend. And despite all the feelings of tenderness and affection, she would never share his religion, nor would he contemplate abandoning his own.

Kumar introduced his friends to his mentor, Professor Smith, who quite often joined in their discussions and contributed his views based on his own observations during the pre-partition days. He was highly impressed with the commitment of these youngsters and once even remarked that God willing, if someday Munir and Kumar or persons of similar inclinations were at the helm of affairs in their respective countries, all problems would be resolved peacefully and there would be an atmosphere of happiness all around.

Two years passed very quickly and it was time for Munir and Gulnar to return to Pakistan for their wedding. Kumar still had one more year to do for his PhD in political science. Since the wedding date had already been set by parents of both Munir and Gulnar, they requested Kumar to be the guest of honour at the wedding. This would also give an opportunity for Kumar to meet all his other old friends. The wedding and all the relevant functions were to take place at Kotri. The lure of visiting his place of birth and memories of love and affection bestowed on him during his childhood were too strong for him not to accept the invitation. He promised that he would definitely be there to take part in all the festivities.

Kumar took two weeks off from his college and reached Kotri a day prior to the wedding. A big surprise awaited him. Shahnawaz had managed using his political clout, to get Kumar's house released from government custody as an evacuee property and had it furnished for his stay during the festivities. Kumar was emotionally so charged that he had to fight hard to hold back his tears when he met Shahnawaz and his wife. In accordance with Kumar's wishes, Shahnawaz called a Hindu priest to perform a short prayer in memory of his parents, which was attended by all the wedding guests. He remembered that dreadful night when he lost both his parents and shed tears in the privacy of his room.

All the wedding functions went very well and everybody enjoyed the wedding celebrations. After the wedding was over, Munir and Gulnar went to Swat and Islamabad for their honeymoon. Kumar decided to visit various parts of Pakistan including the so called Pakistan occupied Kashmir. The view of the natural pristine beauty of Kashmir with its shimmering lakes, lush green valleys, groves of maple, cedar and cypress trees and backdrop of snow-capped mountains was quite breathtaking. His heart filled with joy and pride that it was part of undivided India, his country of birth. The next moment his spell was broken and he was jolted out of his pleasant thoughts, when suddenly at someplace in the distance, a cannon shell exploded followed by a burst of machine gun fire. The little children selling tourist souvenirs and local fruit vendors ran helter-skelter in terror. As usual Indian and Pakistani border forces were engaged in exchanging fire, putting the border villages in danger.

There was a river on the border with a tiny hand-woven rope bridge which linked the two parts of Kashmir in India and Pakistan. Families were not allowed to cross over and had to be content with communicating by shouting across the bridge. An arbitrary line drawn by politicians separated those who had lived there for centuries. He could not imagine the plight of the people living on either side of the border with identical sufferings and clouds of fear. He saw a small grave where a Pakistani soldier killed by Indian bombardment was buried and he was told that across the border there was a monument for an Indian soldier felled by Pakistani bullets. He felt a deep ache in his heart that the life of these young soldiers was snuffed out prematurely in the surroundings of such beauty and tranquility. He cherished life and considered being alive was the greatest gift of nature. He kept asking himself repeatedly how and when this mindless madness would cease and when the human life would be valued more than Indian or Pakistani lands.

This put a dampner on his sightseeing and abruptly cutting short his tour, he came back to Kotri with a heavy heart. After bidding goodbye to Munir's parents and his old friends, Kumar returned to London with a firm resolve to find a way to alleviate the sufferings of both innocent peoples either side of the border.

Kumar's soul became restless as he could not get the suffering of Kashmiris out of his mind. This rekindled the sad memories of his parents who had suffered the similar fate at the hands of religious fanatics. He had not so far known much about this thorny issue, which was tearing the two countries apart. He spent several hours in the library researching archives relating to the United Nation resolutions on the Kashmir issue, to get a deeper understanding of the core problem.

Kumar also had to work hard for his PhD in political science. At the same time Jai-Hind party leader Shankar Singh's daughter Sheila arrived in London to join King's College to study political science under the tutelage of Professor Smith. Sheila was introduced to Kumar by Professor Smith. She was enchanted with Kumar's personality and character but more importantly she empathized very closely with his political views. They spent hours along the banks of the river Thames and looking through the archives in the British library. They researched all available old documents and also shared some lovely moments at coffee houses in London. Kumar was now getting over the heart-breaking memories of his tragic tour of Pakistan occupied Kashmir.

In a few days Munir and Gulnar, now happily married, also

arrived back in London. Munir started working in the oncology (cancer) department at Hammersmith Hospital and soon became quite popular among his patients. He successfully treated high-level dignitaries, ministers and elite members of British aristocracy. His fame spread beyond the boundaries of the country and he started visiting Europe and USA very frequently giving lectures in his specialist subject. Gulnar also became very busy with her sub-editor job with the London Times. In spite of their busy lives they used to meet Kumar few times a month and spent some quality time with him.

Kumar introduced Sheila to Munir and Gulnar and the foursome made a pretty group dedicated to the common ideal of creating peace in the subcontinent. For Kumar, the happy days were back. He now had his old and trusted friends to share his thoughts, frustrations and dreams with. Kumar still pursued his cherished dream of bringing about eternal peace between the two nations.

They generally met at Munir's house or sometimes at the cottage of Professor Smith where his nephew Brian, who was also a classmate of Sheila, would often join them in discussions. Brian had gained his MBA in USA and was now studying political science in London. Brian informed Kumar that during his stay in USA he happened to have a close association with his uncle Lalchand, who now occupied a place of prominence among leading businessmen there. He also told Kumar that Lalchand was contemplating transferring his business to Islamabad, the capital of Pakistan, to pick up the threads of his old business.

Whenever news of any fresh hostility and skirmishes between India and Pakistan made the world headlines, Kumar would burst out:

"Wish I could be the Prime Minister of India."

To which Sheila would riposte emphatically, "Why don't you."

He was startled at such utterances and laughingly used to dismiss the matter. However Sheila was more serious and would assert:

112

"India is a truly democratic country and will allow anyone rich or poor, Hindu or Muslim to occupy the high office as long as he demonstrates his ability to do so together with conviction and devotion to the interests of the nation."

For the first time at this stage Sheila let Kumar know that she belonged to a highly political family, being the daughter of Shankar Singh, head of the political party Jai-Hind, who was being actively considered as a future prime minister. She suggested that if Kumar so desired, they return to India where he could start his political career as one of the top leaders in her father's party as he identified himself with the pain and suffering of the poor. Besides being highly educated, progressive and liberal in his outlook he was also unique, being a Hindu who grew up in Pakistan who had the first-hand knowledge and better understanding of the issues facing the two nations. Topping it all with his really good debating capability that would appeal to the masses, he ticked all the boxes required for becoming a politician that would make a difference in a vast country like India.

One evening, when they all were having tea with Professor Smith at his cottage, the conversation turned to Kumar's entry into politics. It was the general opinion that Kumar along with Sheila should return to India and embark upon a career in politics. Professor Smith, Munir and Gulnar were very encouraging. They felt that the subcontinent needed young blood and fresh ideas to sort out the simmering problems. Munir mentioned that their childhood friend Shahid was very active in Pakistani politics and was aspiring to the high office in that country and therefore Kumar as his counterpart in India would help and solve most issues amicably. Professor Smith volunteered to speak to his old friend and Sheila's father, Shankar, and felt certain he would have no objection to Kumar joining his party and to Kumar's initiation into politics. There was jubilation all around at this happy consensus.

The marriage of Munir and Gulnar was on the rocks. Kumar used to meet them frequently, generally when both were present, but lately quite often he spent more and more time with Gulnar particularly when she was alone during Munir's absence on frequent visits abroad on his professional work. The old passion between them was aroused and fanned further by their being in each other's intimate company at parties, dinners and movies, so much so that even Sheila and Professor Smith suspected that there was more than just platonic friendship between them. Professor Smith, as a friend to both of them, advised Kumar to put a stop to such intimacy.

On the other hand Sheila herself was rather taken with Kumar and wanted to marry him. But Kumar was indecisive. He knew he could not marry Gulnar, because she was already married to his best friend Munir yet he was unable to make his mind up about Sheila.

On return from one of his overseas trips, Munir also heard these rumours of growing closeness between his wife and his best friend and was truly disturbed. That night Gulnar lovingly broke the news to Munir that she was pregnant with his child but Munir accused her of carrying the child of Kumar. In spite of strong denials from both Gulnar and Kumar, Munir decided to pack off Gulnar back to her father's place in Pakistan. He continued his friendship with Kumar due to the intervention of Professor Smith, but it lacked the warmth and amity of the old. One evening, in a fit of rage, in the presence of Professor Smith, Brian and Sheila, he openly accused Kumar of shattering his marriage and swore that sooner or later he would get even with him.

This absurd accusation by Munir spurred Kumar in making up his mind to marry Sheila. He thought it was the the best way to avoid any misunderstandings. He proposed to Sheila and asked if she would marry him. She was of course delighted. Sheila informed her father Shankar, who gave her his blessings but suggested that they should get married in London. He would not be able to attend the wedding as he would be preoccupied with the upcoming elections. They also got blessings from Professor Smith. They were married at a Registrar's office in a simple ceremony which only Brian and Professor Smith attended. Munir was conspicuous by his absence at the ceremony.

Soon Kumar and Sheila both completed their PhDs and with

the encouragement of Professor Smith, they decided to return to India. Sheila informed her father of their arrival date in Delhi, who was delighted.

Shankar Singh, Sheila's father, with his entourage was present at the Indira Gandhi International airport to receive them. There were large crowds who had assembled to welcome the daughter of their popular leader and her spouse. Kumar wondered whether his decision to return to India at that time was proper. He did not expect such a chaotic and frenzied reception on arrival and was very much distressed. Sheila, who was used to seeing such masses of crowds for her father, grasped Kumar's hand firmly and gave it a tight squeeze to reassure him that everything would settle down eventually.

The next few weeks were crowded with the formal celebration of their marriage, introduction to family members, relatives and Jai-Hind party leaders. They were invited to numerous dinner parties and finally a pilgrimage to the holy shrines and the holy Ganges at Varanasi to invoke divine blessings to launch Kumar's political career.

Varanasi, also commonly known as Banaras or Kashi, is a city on the banks of river Ganges in the Indian state of Uttar Pradesh about two hundred miles from the state capital Lucknow. It is regarded as a holy city by Hindus. Hindus believe that death at Varanasi can bring salvation. Varanasi is today considered to be the spiritual capital of India. A dip in the holy Ganges is regarded very sacred and it is believed it gives people success in their mission.

Shankar Singh, the president of Jai-Hind party started coaching Kumar in the ways of Indian politics. Kumar with his high education in political science was readily accepted in the party circles. However within three months of giving his best to the party as a hard working young man, he was disillusioned that his own secular ideology, political integrity and transparency and sympathy towards the suffering of the down trodden were being compromised and were at total variance with his father-in-law's style of running the party. He realised that his father-in-law was corrupted by power and the party had two faces. One face was for retaining power at any cost and the other lining the pockets of party leaders without any consideration to the needs of the people. He decided to leave the Jai-Hind party as soon as possible.

He discussed his issues with Sheila, who was quite understanding about his frustration with the party. However she cautioned him that until such time as he established himself as a leader in his own right, he would have to maintain a working relationship with Shankar Singh and his party. Kumar concurred with Sheila's views and he worked tirelessly with the poor, the downtrodden and the under-privileged. His oratory skills came in very handy as he knew how, when and what to say to the people. His message was clear and concise and his policies sound and appealing. He advocated peace at home and abroad and particularly with immediate neighbours; preventing waste of national resources and eradication of corruption. National wealth was meant to be spent for the betterment of the common man rather than being invested in futile projects for the benefit of a few selected persons.

The general public liked his ideas and he gained popularity with the masses as a young leader with fresh and novel ideas. Two years passed very quickly and Kumar now felt that the time was ripe to separate from the Jai-Hind party. In fact Shankar Singh himself was jittery. Shankar was getting worried about Kumar's increasing personal popularity with the masses and began viewing him as a grave threat to his own leadership. Kumar with his supporters, floated a new party called Satya, the name itself reflecting his mission of truth.

Kumar with Sheila's support set out to achieve his goal. He brought entirely new concepts to Indian politics; accepting supremacy of human life above land; accepting people's right to self-determination; respecting dissent; equality and dignity of all human beings irrespective of their poverty or low occupation. His party placed greater emphasis on building bridges with neighbouring countries, settling disputes amicably without resorting to violent means and bringing about a lasting peace throughout the subcontinent.

116

His concepts spread all over like wild fire. Having grown weary of the politics of hatred and violence ever since the independence, the people long awaited for the emergence of an apostle (avtar) with a message of peace. Hundreds of thousands of Indians residing abroad heard him over the television, read about him in the papers and believed in his manifesto. Hundreds of volunteers from all over the world descended on India to lend support to his party. The world community endorsed the policies of Satya party, who started gearing up for the general elections to the Indian Parliament (Lok Sabha) scheduled in two month's time.

Shankar Singh, himself an aspirant of the prime ministerial position was alarmed by the results of pre-poll surveys and tried to prevail upon his daughter Sheila to dissuade Kumar from contesting the elections in direct opposition to him. Kumar should instead merge Satya party with Jai-Hind party so that with their joint strength they would easily capture political power, he suggested.

Shankar assured Sheila that he would make Kumar his Deputy Prime Minister with important portfolios. Kumar would have full autonomy and support to pursue his goals. Sheila discussed the matter with Kumar, who having known the political manoeuvers of Shankar pointedly refused to have any political or electoral collaboration with Jai-Hind party. This created a rift in their relationship, so much so that Sheila started canvassing in the elections for her father and the Jai-Hind party.

Kumar did not get disheartened. He decided to soldier on with his crusade in his campaign for election. He travelled all over the links and breadth of India from Kashmir in the north to the southern tip of India, Knayakumari. Knayakumari is famed for its incomparable geographical location of its lands end of India where the Arabian Sea, the Indian Ocean and the Bay of Bengal all meet. It is in the state of Tamilnadu. He also travelled from Bengal in the east across to Gujarat in the west.

He covered all the states of India giving the same message to

117

make India prosper and create peace in the subcontinent. Multitudes of people flocked everywhere to listen to his messages.

It came as no surprise to political pundits and stalwarts of the nation that the Satya party swept the polls securing 400 seats from the total strength of Lok Sabha 552 seats. It was well over the minimum requirement to gain absolute majority in the Lok Sabha. Kumar was unanimously elected leader of the Satya party and was invited by the President of India to form the government.

Since Kumar had lived his childhood years in Pakistan, he never made any secret of his desire to create a condition of peaceful co-existence between the two countries. It was rumoured that he would give priority to finding an early solution to end hostilities with Pakistan. He had repeatedly asserted at his public meetings during the election campaign that far too many wars had been waged between the two neighbours ever since the partition and it was time that more concerted efforts were made to put a permanent end to these hostilities.

As per schedule, Kumar and his cabinet were administered the oath of office by the President of India at Rashtrapti Bhavan. In a short speech after being sworn in, Kumar reiterated his resolve to try for an eternal peace with Pakistan and announced that he would make a major policy statement in that regard at his first public rally in six month's time. He promised to hold serious consultations with his cabinet colleagues, his party leaders and even with the leaders of opposition parties during the interim period to seek their support for the steps he intended to take to implement the policy.

A big rally was organised in the vast Ambedkar stadium after six months of discussions with all the parties and cabinet. It was attended by the Indian public at large as well as a number of foreign nationals, diplomats and distinguished visitors from other countries specially invited for this occasion. A high security enclosure was provided to seat foreign invitees including visiting heads of states. There were members of cabinet, their spouses and leaders of the ruling and opposition parties. Also seated in this enclosure was Kumar's uncle Lalchand who was now settled in US. Also present were Brian, Professor's Smith's nephew who was now working for The British High Commission. Brian had brought his video camera to capture the whole speech and was given a seat in the front row at the request of Sheila and had a vantage position for filming. There was a mass presence of press and television crews for the live telecast of this rally.

Kumar walked up to the podium to announce his keenly awaited policy of peace, but before he could say anything, he was shot down. Sheila was aghast and ran to the podium along with security forces to attend to Kumar. Police and security forces surrounded the stadium. They frisked all the visitors in the enclosure, but no weapon was found except for a solitary licensed gun in Sheila's handbag, which she was always permitted to carry as part of her security. No one dared to question the Prime Minister's wife in her hour of grief. The police however took possession of the gun for forensic tests. Kumar was taken to All India Institute of Medical Sciences along with Sheila to have immediate treatment.

Munir and Gulnar landed at the Delhi airport, the same time as Professor Smith's plane touched down at the airport. They took a taxi directly to the hospital where Kumar was being treated. They were allowed entry to the restricted intensive care unit after Sheila who was already there, vouched for them. They found Kumar in a very critical condition and doctors told them that he was on his last breaths. As if waiting to bid final goodbye to his friends and mentor, with great difficulty Kumar opened his eyes momentarily to greet them with a tortured smile and then with an agonising sigh of disappointment he closed his eyes, never to open them again.

The sad news of his death went out to the grieving masses assembled outside and to the unbelieving and shocked world that another apostle of peace had left this world. One more life in the cause of peace had been sacrificed. A state funeral was scheduled after three days. Kumar's body was kept in state at his residence for the mourners to pay their last respects.

119

A high level team of investigators was constituted to probe the assassination. Since it was considered to be a political killing, virtually everyone who was seated in the high security enclosure at the time of the shooting was interrogated. They also made inquiries regarding his close friends who were with him at college in London. They started with Munir. It came to light that Munir had threatened Kumar because of an alleged affair with his wife Gulnar and he might have hired a hit man. Munir explained the entire situation to the investigators. He told them that it was true that he was upset with Kumar because of his suspicion, but he had long since cleared his differences with Kumar and Sheila knows about it. On return to Pakistan his wife Gulnar had DNA test for the baby. The tests conclusively proved that baby was Munir's and not Kumar's. Munir had sent a letter of apology to Kumar and everything was cleared. Sheila vouched for this and said that relations between Kumar and Munir had been very cordial since then. Munir also told investigators that he agreed with the policies of Kumar as he too wanted peace between Pakistan and India. He would not dream of harming Kumar in any way. Gulnar also confirmed that relations between Kumar and Munir were now very friendly as previously. The investigators seemed satisfied with Munir's explanations but advised him that he should stay in India till their investigation was completed.

Meanwhile a confidential report was sent to the investigators proving that the ballistics test had shown that the fatal bullet was fired from Sheila's gun. This was conveyed to the acting prime minister, who went to meet Sheila and wanted her reaction regarding access to her gun. Sheila was aghast and requested the acting prime minister to give her some time to try to recollect who could have had access to her gun. She was sure that she had not let the gun out of her possession at any time. She was certain that it was all the time in her handbag right from the instant she left their house to attend the rally, until the time when police took it from her handbag.

The investigators next concentrated their focus on Kumar's uncle Lalchand. They found out that after settling down with his business in USA, Lalchand had come in contact with the CIA. The CIA was looking out for a person of substance to be deployed as an undercover agent in India with the main objective of ensuring that India and Pakistan continued to remain at loggerheads on every issue. USA had political and commercial reasons for keeping India and Pakistan away from any peace moves, specially the Kashmir issue. There was no better person than Lalchand who being of Indian origin could travel freely to Pakistan and India. He had useful business and political links in both countries. The CIA struck a deal with Lalchand to work for USA interests in India in return for USA administration ensuring him a trading monopoly for consumer items.

A businessman like Lalchand could not let go this lucrative opportunity and re-established his business in Islamabad. He worked as an undercover agent for the CIA, his main job being to ensure that India and Pakistan remained enemies. When the Satya party became popular and was likely to win the elections, he questioned Kumar at the behest of CIA regarding his policies towards Pakistan. Kumar very candidly and unreservedly reaffirmed his faith in a lasting peace between India and Pakistan, a desire he had nurtured since his childhood.

Lalchand conveyed these views to his American masters who asked him to try any means to ensure that Kumar's Satya party did not win the elections. The CIA financed all his measures to prevent Kumar from succeeding at the polls. They went as far as to instruct him to eliminate Kumar if necessary. Investigators managed to get all the truth out of Lalchand who confessed that he was a CIA agent but had no hand in the killing of Kumar. He just could not pick up the courage to kill his own nephew.

Investigators next turned attention to Shankar Singh the leader of the Jai-Hind party, the father-in-law of Kumar and his main adversary in the elections. Shankar Singh was frantically against any compromise with Pakistan. He confessed that he was not happy with the peace talks and had been approached by Lalchand on behalf of the CIA to oppose any peace moves with Pakistan. He had agreed that he was opposed to any peace initiatives with Pakistan but categorically denied having engineered Kumar's assassination nor did he have any hand in the killing of Kumar and in any event he had no access to Sheila's gun.

That led investigators to the last suspect Brian. He was in college with Kumar, Sheila, Munir and Gulnar. After finishing college in London he was now working for The British High Commission in Delhi. Since Brian had known Kumar and Sheila since their college days, he was a frequent visitor to their house. With his increasing workload Kumar could not devote much time to Sheila. Feeling neglected, Sheila grew closer to Brian, who had become her constant companion. He would escort Sheila to social events, political meetings and would have dinners together all the time, though under the watchful eyes of the security guards assigned to the Prime Minister. Kumar heard the rumours but ignored them. He had full faith in Sheila and his friend Brian. On the contrary he felt happy that Sheila had good company to keep her engaged as he personally hardly got any time to spend with her.

Brian, taking advantage of being a special guest, started snooping in affairs of the state. RAW the secret agency of India warned Kumar about Brian. Kumar confronted Brian about it which he emphatically denied. Sheila tried to calm Kumar down but Kumar would not budge.

The investigators shifted all their attention now to Brian, who claimed diplomatic immunity. He said in his defence that there was no evidence that he had any access to Sheila's gun and besides there was no forensic evidence found which could implicate him. RAW had indirectly found out that Brian was also a CIA agent. This investigation came to an impasse. Investigators were convinced that Brian had shot Kumar but could not prove it. This became quite like the American President John Kennedy assassination case where no conclusive evidence was found.

Three days after the assassination the funeral took place with full State honours. An eerie silence descended over the entire city and people only talked in whispers. The entire route from the prime minister's residence to a specially erected funeral pyre on the banks of the river Yamuna was lined with thousands of grieving and sobbing people. The state funeral of Kumar was in progress. The procession was conducted appropriately with grace and dignity. Sheila, Kumar's widow, along with Munir, Gulnar and Professor Smith walked just behind Kumar's flag draped casket on a gun carriage. The Indian air force aircraft scattered rose petals.

Munir lit the pyre while the priests recited Vedic hymns. In the flickering light of the pyre fire, the sight of the ashen face of Sheila brought tears to every eye. The nation bade a tearful farewell to one of its most worthy sons. There was one question on every person's lips: How many more Kumars will need to be sacrificed in the pursuit of peace in the subcontinent?

The law of sacrifice is uniform
throughout the world
To be effective
it demands the sacrifice
Of the bravest
and the most spotless

Mahatma Gandhi

The 8th Colour of the rainbow

The lifeless body of Kailash lay on a small platform covered with wooden sandalwood sticks. A red vermillion dot had been applied to his forehead. The yellow dahlia flowers placed all around him gave out a pleasant fragrance. His widow in a white sari and devoid of the traditional vermillion in the parting of her hair, stood by pensively with her small child. His father was present there in white clothes. There was a red glow of sunset in the west with a cool breeze blowing from Yamuna. No rich and famous dignitaries were present to pay their respects, but there was a long line of ordinary people and half-clad workers for whom Kailash had given his life. They all knew that there would be no statue erected for him because he was not a famous leader or politician. But he will always live in their hearts. He had a smile on his face suggesting that he was happier now than when he was alive.

Kailash Gohil was born in Porbandar, a coastal city in the western Indian state of Gujarat, perhaps best known for being the birthplace of Mahatma Gandhi and Sudhama, a destitute friend of Lord Krishna. He had no recollection of his early days. His father left Porbandar when Kailash was seven years old and the family moved to Rajkot. Rajkot is the fourth largest city in the state of Gujarat, after Ahmedabad, Surat and Vadodra and much larger than Porbandar. It has a population of more than 1.6 million. The city is 245 kilometers from the state capital Gandhinagar.

Kailash was very shy but a very honest person. He never uttered a lie either to his school teachers or his fellow pupils. His books were his sole companions. Kailash's father, Mohan Das Gohil was a judge at the local court and was reputed as being a man of sound principles and robust integrity who could not be bribed by anybody. He always taught his son also to be honest in dealing with anybody he came in contact with.

Kailash turned out to be a brilliant student at college. He won over the confidence of his teachers and became their blue-eyed boy. He went on to obtain a scholarship for outstanding performance in the English subject. He cleared his BA degree in Economics. His success, however was marred by the company of spoiled rich friends. He fell into a habit of smoking. Though he did not quite like smoking, he did get much pleasure in forming and emitting rings and clouds of smoke from his mouth. By tradition, most Gujaratis are vegetarians but Kailash started eating meat being influenced by the company of his friends. Since meat was never cooked in their house, he started eating outside in restaurants with his friends. If that was not enough, he started enjoying alcoholic drinks. His friends came from affluent families and did not mind splurging money for his drinks and good life.

Kailash was being thoroughly spoiled by his friends. To celebrate the success at the BA exams, his friends gave him a special treat. They took him to a brothel in Rajkot. They sent Kailash in with the necessary instructions. It was all pre-arranged and the bill had already been paid. He went into the jaws of sin but God, in his infinite mercy, protected him from himself. Kailash was almost struck blind and dumb in this den of vice. He sat near the woman on her bed but was tongue-tied. She eventually lost patience with him and showed him the door, hurling abuses and insults at him. He felt as though his manhood had been hurt and wished he fell into a deep abyss for shame. But Kailash was always grateful to God for having been saved by the skin of his teeth from this misadventure.

All these vices now began to weigh heavily on Kailash's conscience, and he decided to make a clean breast of it and make a confession to his father. He was certain that it would cause his father a lot of pain, but he had to take that risk because he believed there could be no cleansing without a confession. He could not summon up enough courage to face and speak directly to his father so he decided to write instead. In his confession, not only he admitted to his guilt and vices, but he also asked his father for forgiveness and pleaded for adequate punishment to be meted out to him as a judge would in a court of law. Kailash's father used to sit in the study at his home in the evenings. Kailash with his hands trembling handed over his confession to his father in the study and sat in a chair opposite. His father read it through, tear drops trickling down his cheeks like the pearl-drops, which he dabbed away with a handkerchief. For a moment he closed his eyes and went into deep thought. He later tore up the confession note. Kailash could see his father's agony, and he too found it hard to hold back his own tears. This memory had always remained etched vividly in his mind.

Those pearl-drops of love cleansed Kailash's heart and he felt his sins washed away. Only he who has experienced such love will understand it. Only he who is smitten with the arrows of love knows its power.

This sort of sublime forgiveness was not natural to Kailash's father. He was wonderfully peaceful, due to Kailash's clean confession. A clean confession, combined with a promise never to commit these sins again, in his view, was the purest form of repentance.

The time had arrived for Kailash to make his mind up about what he should do after he obtained his BA degree. He wanted to be a teacher, but his father Mohan Das wished Kailash to attend law school. Mohan Das suggested Kailash sat in his court as an observer for the next few days so that he could get an insight into the process of law. His father hoped that this might also help Kailash in making up his mind about choosing law as his career.

Kailash was at a stage in his life that was highly impressionable. He was an extremely sensitive individual who had special feelings and pains for others who were downtrodden and deprived. One day a woman with a soiled and torn sari and dishevelled hair appeared in the court. She was trying hard to hold back her tears, and her eyes were red. Two little children were tugging at her sari, and their eyes had an expression of unknown fear. During the proceedings Kailash learned that her husband was killed in an ambush in the middle of one night. The prosecutor explained that a builder wanted to build an apartment complex but a small mud house belonging to this woman and her husband was interfering with his plans. Apparently, many attempts, fair and foul, were made to dislodge this fellow but he refused every time. The builder with his unlimited resources and connections with police arranged to have him bumped off. The builder was sitting in the court with sneer on his face and disrespect for this grieving family.

In spite of every sincere effort on the part of the prosecutor, the builder's defence team were able to arrange a number of false witnesses who were successful in proving that the beleaguered widow was a liar. She cried, she raised her hand to the judge and to all those present, in an appeal for mercy, but against the huge conspiracy she was helpless. Kailash noticed that though his father was very sympathetic towards her and even believed her version of events, but on the basis of evidence, presented before him he had to decide against her. He saw the woman holding hands of her two innocent children walk away with an unsteady gait through the door into a dark future.

This incidence made an ever-lasting impression on Kailash's mind. A wave of intense abhorrence towards this corrupt society and the wide network of conspiracies which had engulfed India at large heaved heavily in his chest. He decided that not only will he adopt law as his career but make it his work ethos to do his utmost to defend such helpless and downtrodden people and uproot the corruption from his beloved country.

Kailash was now more than happy to accord with his father's wishes and adopt law as his career. Mohan Das wanted to send Kailash to London to study the law. His father was quite happy to bear all his expenses because Kailash was his only son and he wanted to do the best for him. Mohan Das wanted Kailash to become a barrister and practice law in India. He had many friends in London and he would give letter of introduction to Kailash so that he had no distractions and could pursue his studies in England without any hindrances.

Kailash's mother was not happy with her husband's decision. She shuddered at the mere thought of Kailash going away from her for so many years. Mohan Das tried to convince his wife but she was still averse to the idea. Someone had told her that young men easily go astray in the western world. They begin to eat meat, drink liquor, smoke and come back to India with a *gori mem* (white woman). Kailash urged his mother to have trust in him. As she knew he never lied and had solemnly pledged to her that he will keep away from such things, she relented and agreed.

Kailash now had to have his passport made along with a visa for England. He filled in the application for a passport and came to Mumbai to submit it to the passport office as there were no such facilities in Rajkot. He was told that it would take at least six weeks for the passport to get ready. Three months passed and still there was no sign of his passport. He decided to go back to Mumbai and make enquiries regarding the delay. He was told that there were lots of applications being processed and it will still take further time. He was getting tired sitting at home in Rajkot with no work or college to go to. As he came out of passport office, a man met him, who suggested that if he paid one thousand rupees, he would be able to get the passport for him by next day. Kailash was astounded that after nearly seventy years of independence, the bribery was still rife in India so blatantly.

Kailash did not want to pay this bribe but he was getting desperate to go to England and saw no other option than to pay up but he made a firm resolve in his mind that when he returned from London after acquiring the law degree, he will make every effort to root out the evil of corruption in India. How can a lone person fight against corruption in India when it runs so deep in Indian blood. Yet he resolved to find a way to hit at the very heart of the corrupt system in India. But little did he know that to get rid of corruption from India is like extracting just one single drop of pure water from an ocean.

Kailash got his passport the very next day after paying one thousand rupees to that man. The corrupt people are very good at keeping their promises. The next step for Kailash was to fill in his application for a student visa at the British High Commission. He was told that it could take up to four weeks to get the visa. He was however pleasantly surprised when he received his visa in three weeks and that too without any bribe. Though the British were in India for two centuries they had not adopted the Indian malaise of corruption, he mused reflectively.

Kailash with blessings from his father and permission from his mother began preparing to set off for England. He had to equip himself for the journey. He got clothes and other things ready. The necktie, which he would be delighted in wearing later on, he abhorred at that time.

The day came at last when he boarded the plane from Mumbai airport for London. His father came to see him off and wished him good luck reminding him of his promise given to his mother to refrain from adopting bad habits. Kailash had not forgotten his promise and vowed again to keep to his word.

This was his first journey in an aircraft and also the first one overseas. He had a window seat. He was fascinated by the clouds and the plane going through them. He knew and wondered about the miracles of modern technology and man's achievements to touch the sky but he still understood man's limitations against supremacy of nature.

Kailash had an Englishman sitting next to him in the plane. He requested a vegetarian meal while the Englishman ordered a non - vegetarian meal. The Englishman introduced himself as Peter Smith and casually mentioned to Kailash that it is so cold in England that one cannot possibly live there without eating meat. Kailash replied that he had heard that there are lots of vegetarians living in England and lead very healthy lives, besides he also mentioned to Peter that he was bound by a solemn promise to his parents that he will not touch meat, so he cannot even think of it and was determined to remain vegetarian throughout his life. Kailash went on to say, that he was fairly confident that he will survive in England without consuming meat.

Mr Patel, for whom his father had given an introduction letter, was at the Heathrow airport to meet Kailash. Mr Patel had made arrangements for Kailash to stay as a paying guest with an English family with a view to him gaining experience of the British way of life and customs. His food however posed a serious problem. He could not relish bland boiled vegetables cooked without condiment or Indian spices. Consequently bread and spinach became his staple diet. The host getting disgusted with this state of affairs said to Kailash that it was silly to remain vegetarian because of a promise he had made to his parents. But Kailash was adamant and said, "A vow is vow and cannot be broken." Then one day he had a stroke of luck He visited Wembley and Southall and found plenty vegetarian restaurants where he was also able to get take away vegetarian food. Besides he found all sorts of Indian groceries available in many supermarkets. He would buy and keep food in the fridge which he would warm in microwave oven whenever he desired. Now Kailash turned his attention to the main purpose for which he had come to London, that was to attain law degree.

Kailash applied at Cambridge University for his law degree. Studying law at Cambridge is hard work but it is one of the most stimulating, interesting and highly regarded courses you could hope to take at the university. Although the course at Cambridge is primarily concerned with English law, there are opportunities to study international law. Indian law is mainly modelled on English law with some modifications. Most law graduates intend to practice law as barristers or solicitors and Cambridge is prominent in both these branches of legal profession.

Kailash managed to get admission to King's College Cambridge to study law. It was a three year course which has two parts, and you must pass exams in both parts to obtain an honours degree.

With still some time to go before commencement of his course at Cambridge, Kailash decided to visit Paris because he was not sure that he may get the time after graduation to visit this part of the world again. He was also fascinated by the Channel Tunnel. It is a 50.5 kilometer long undersea rail tunnel linking Folkstone Kent in the UK to Calais in France. The tunnel carries high-speed Eurostar passenger trains, Eurotunnel shuttle vehicle transport - the largest international rail freight trains in the world.

Ideas for a cross-channel fixed link were first mooted in 1802 but British politicians amid fears that it might result in compromised national security stalled the construction of a tunnel. Eventually construction began in 1988 and the tunnel opened commercially in 1994. The Channel Tunnel consists of three tunnels: two tunnels carry the trains and a smaller middle tunnel is used as service tunnel. It takes 35 minutes to travel across the Channel Tunnel, from terminal to terminal. Kailash went by northern tunnel from England to France and returned to England by the southern tunnel from France. It cost him £100 which he thought it was well worth it to see Tunnel technology at its best.

Kailash's main interest in Paris was the Eiffel Tower. Constructed entirely of iron, the tower stands nearly 1000 feet high. It is named after the engineer Gustave Eiffel whose company built the tower in the year 1889. It is the tallest structure in Paris and has become the most prominent landmark of Paris, also seen often in the establishing shot of movies set in the city. He ascended it three times and there was a restaurant on the first platform which also served vegetarian food. Kailash had lunch at that restaurant, just for the satisfaction that he had food at a great height, though it cost him a pretty penny in Euro currency. Kailash also visited the ancient churches of Paris. He found their grandeur awesome. The wonderful construction of Notre Dame and its elaborate interior decoration with beautiful sculptures he found were magnificent.

Kailash came back to London very refreshed but a little poorer in his money reserves. Still he felt very contented that Paris trip would always be one of his cherished memories. Now it was time for him to get to the grind and commence his studies at Cambridge. The word 'law' usually conjures up either a graphic snapshot of the more sensational murders, rapes and other violent crimes that grab headlines of the tabloid press, or the depressing image of balding, middle-aged men in grey pin-striped city suits worrying about making wrong statements in press and at work. Neither picture is wholly wrong, but both are inadequate.

Law is indeed about drama and conflict, of the individual and the society. It is also about rigorous logic, care and precision, clarity of thought and attention to detail. The law is not an easy ticket to being a fat cat. It can also be an absorbing, passionate and very satisfying way of spending a working life.

Cambridge is accepted as having one of the strongest law faculties in the country covering the core subjects of criminal law which you will need wherever you practice law. Kailash was interested in studying law at Cambridge to fight against corruption in India. He was aware that people with money got away with murder in India by devious and unscrupulous ways. He was determined to fight corruption by becoming a prosecuting lawyer and bring perpetrators of corruption to justice. He knew his father had a reputation of being an honest judge and he wanted to follow in his footsteps.

King's College Cambridge focussed on encouraging students to think critically about the role of law within the political, economic and moral systems, as well as mastering the necessary tools of legal reasoning and analysis. The college library was well-stocked with law books and remained open 24/7 for students to study in peace and quiet. You need a clear logical mind, a willingness to think through rationally to argue a case. The ability to speak coherently and precisely is vital to succeed in this profession.

Kailash was very happy at Cambridge. It was a city with lot of

133

greenery. Though it is a bike city and lots of students cycle around all day, you can walk about and get the fresh air of countryside. The course had only few lectures every week but he had to study more at the library to complete modules and project work.

Kailash was very impressed with the discipline and dedication of teachers at King's College. Unlike in India, here they were very helpful and always there to assist and advise. He found it tough going but at the same time very stimulating and interesting. He used to spend a lot of time in the library.

Kailash was a friendly person and soon made lots of friends both male and female. It helped him improve his English and also gave him a better understanding of his law course. He was able to understand the actual subject rather than memorizing which is done commonly in Indian colleges. One thing did surprise him though that the girl students once they become friendly with their fellow students had no inhibitions in spending nights with them in their rooms and vice versa without any restriction which he found very strange because it is unthinkable in India. A lot of girls were very willing and happy to come to his room during the day as well at night but he had a lot of self-control and was bound by his promise to his parents that he will not bring a *gori mem* from England. He did miss his parents especially his mother but thanks to modern technology he was able to talk to her on Skype frequently. He was also able to keep in touch with his father and friends via e-mail, another marvel of modern communication where letters reach within seconds to other people via computer.

Three years passed. Kailash passed his law degree with flying colours. Kailash now had to complete the purpose for which he had come to England. It was for being called to the Bar. There were two conditions which had to be fulfilled before a student was formally called to the Bar: Keeping terms, twelve terms equivalent to about three years, and passing further examinations. Keeping terms meant attending at least six out of about twenty-four dinners in a term. Eating did not actually mean partaking of the dinner, it meant reporting oneself at the fixed hours and remaining present throughout the dinner.

Kailash often ate nothing at these dinners because to his dismay hardly any vegetarian dishes were served there.

Two bottles of wine were allowed to each group of four and as Kailash did not touch wine, he was always in demand in his group of four. You had to pay, however, a fair amount of money to attend these dinners. He could not see how these dinners prepared the students any better for the Bar. But he realised later that these occasions helped to give them knowledge of the world with a sort of polish and refinement and also improved their skills of speaking. The institution had gradually lost all its meaning, but conservative England has still retained it. Barristers are humorously known as 'dinner barristers'. He was called to the Bar after clearing his exams and was enrolled as a barrister in the High Court.

Kailash had no intention of practicing law in England for long, he just wanted to have some work experience in England before he returned home to become a crusader against corruption in India. He also wanted to see few famous attractions in London before he headed back to India as he thought it highly unlikely he will get to visit England again anytime soon. He joined the King's Bench Walk Inner Temple college as a pupilage. He worked under Mr Simon Ward QC who trained him well and he also let him argue the cases in High Court under his supervision.

Kailash first visited the world renowned Madam Tussaud's wax museum near Baker Street. He was fascinated by the lifelike statues of various personalities from around the World. He was impressed to see a statue of the first Indian, Mahatma Gandhi. Statues of other famous Indians were added subsequently at regular intervals including movie stars like Amitabh Bachchan and Shah Rukh Khan and cricket legend Sachin Tendulkar. He also saw the statues of Queen Elizabeth and various American presidents including Abraham Lincoln and Barack Obama. He could not help but admire the sincere efforts of the artists in creating living and dead legends which looked very real.

Kailash next visited the Tower of London. It was built by

135

William the Conqueror in 1078. It was used as a prison since year 1100, though that was not its primary purpose. These days it serves as a home to the Royal Mint and Crown Jewels of the United Kingdom. In medieval times executions of traitors were commonly held on the notorious Tower Hill to the north of the castle. It is cared for by the charity 'Historic Royal Palaces' and protected as a World Heritage Site. He found it interesting to see torture chambers and Crown Jewels. He also saw the Tower Bridge built around year 1886 and London Bridge and also originally made in 19th century but lately replaced by a new one in 1973. London is demarcated by River Thames into north and south and these two bridges help the motorists and pedestrians.

Next on Kailash's list was a visit to the flood barrier built on River Thames. It is the world's second largest moveable flood barrier (first is in Netherlands) and is located downstream of central London. London is vulnerable to floods and heavy tides. A storm surge generated by low pressure in the Atlantic Ocean is funneled down the North Sea which narrows the English Channel and the Thames estuary. If the storm surge combines with spring tide, dangerously high water levels can occur in the Thames estuary. This situation combined with downstream flows in the Thames provides the triggers for flood defence operations.

The Thames Barrier has been operational since 1982. When needed it is closed during high tide; at low tide it can be opened to enhance the river's flow towards the sea. There was a flood in the Thames in 1928 when fourteen people had died. The concept of the rotating gates was devised by Charles Draper and was designed by Rendel, Palmer and Tritton of Greater London Council. It is built across 520-meter wide stretch of river and its construction cost around £534 million. It is predicted to last up to year 2030. Kailash was fascinated by this awesome looking engineering marvel.

His sightseeing continued with a visit to the London Eye. It is a giant Ferris wheel situated on the southern bank of the River Thames in the vicinity Westminster Bridge. The entire structure is 135 meters tall and the wheel has a diameter of 120 meters. Construction started in

1998 and completed in March 2000. It is the world's tallest cantilevered observation wheel. On average the London Eye receives more visitors per year than the Taj Mahal and the Great Pyramids of Egypt. The 32 capsules on the London Eye represent 32 London boroughs and each weighs as much as 1,052,631 pound coins. The London Eye can carry 800 people each rotation which is comparable to 11 London red double decker buses. The capsules travel at a leisurely pace of 26 cm per second, which is twice as fast as a tortoise sprinting. Kailash was very lucky when he took a ride in the London Eye. It was a clear day and he was able to see up to a distance of 40 kilometers in all directions as far as Windsor Castle. He was glad that he had a ride in London Eye considering it has become an important landmark and an iconic structure in London.

Meanwhile working as a pupilage barrister, Kailash became very popular. His winning success rate was nearly 90% and his boss Simon Ward was very pleased with his work. After completion of his nine months as a pupilage, Mr Ward offered Kailash a three year contract to work for the firm. Soon Kailash became a well-known name in his own right in the legal circles in London. His reputation of being honest and sincere made him famous in a short time. Kailash often used to take and represent the cases for needy clients as pro-bono without any fee. Three years passed very quickly and Kailash started feeling homesick though he was in regular touch with his parents by phone, e-mail and Skype. He now desired female company. There were lots of willing English and Indian girls, who wanted to go out with him but he did not want to break his promise given to his parents that he would not marry a girl from England. He was duty bound to get married in India to an Indian girl. He gave a formal notice to Mr Ward that he will leave at the end of his three year contract. Mr Ward was very sorry to lose him but agreed that his talents will be more beneficial to his own community in India and wished him good luck and gave him a well deserved send-off party.

England is a small island but there are so many historical places and so much else to see that you need few months to see it all. Kailash's friends had told him that they had lived in England for many years yet they have not been able to see many of these places. Kailash had no more time left to stay in London, besides his mother was not in good health and kept imploring him that he returned home after completing his law degree and once he had gained good experience of practicing law in England. He was very sad on having to leave London. He bid farewell to London with tearful eyes but he carried with him fond memories of London with lots of photographs to share with his family and friends.

Kailash came back to Rajkot via Mumbai. His mother was delirious at seeing him and especially that he had kept his word and not brought a white wife from London. Mohan Das Gohil was also very proud of his son who had achieved the coveted law degree from Cambridge. He advised Kailash to look for an appropriate job. Mohan Das told Kailash that he had maintained absolute honesty in his professional career and expected Kailash to do the same. Mohan Das did warn him that there is lot of corruption in Indian legal system including many judges who are corrupt. Kailash must practice law with honesty and integrity as he had learned at Cambridge. The people of India have appointed the judges to provide justice and discharge duties according to law. They have been appointed as gods and not as devils. He should not allow such devils to continue. His honesty might seem like a drop in the ocean but it may bring awakening otherwise it will spell doom for the judiciary. Kailash promised to his father that he will do his best to follow in his footsteps and practice law with conscience. Since he had qualified as a barrister, he applied for a job at a few law firms in Delhi

Meanwhile his mother was now very keen to get Kailash married. She felt that since he is applying to practice in Delhi and will be away from Rajkot most of the time, he will feel lonesome. Besides she wanted him to get married so that she can have grandchildren to enjoy and care for. Kailash agreed that he would be happy to be introduced to suitable girls. He wanted a simple good looking girl with a soul sparkling through her eyes. Kailash's mother Savitri was very pleased and promised him that she will keep that in mind.

Kailash met a few girls introduced to him by his mother. He found most of them too fast and too modern for his liking. But when he met Simran, his heart was singing and the bells started to ring. Simran had blue eyes and he wanted to dive into the depth of those ocean blue eyes. He wanted to seek out pearls hidden inside them. Kailash told Simran that he was able to see her soul in eyes and that her voice had the sweetness of Sarswati tunes. Simran was equally impressed by Kailash and his simple nature and mild demeanour. She also fell in love with Kailash and told him that he had touched her heart. It looked like it was love at first sight for both of them. Kailash told Simran that he had crossed the oceans of time to find her and that he had fallen head over heels in love with her. Simran replied that she had touched the skies and their hearts were singing the same tune and they will not part until death.

When Kailash told her mother about Simran and how he had fallen in love with her, his mother was very excited and decided to contact Simran's parents to ask her hand for Kailash. Simran also told her parents about Kailash and of her willingness to marry him. Her parents were very pleased and wanted to meet Kailash's parents. In spite of modern times both Kailash and Simran were happy for their parents to meet and arrange their marriage. Kailash told his mother that Simran was as pure as fresh dew drops and not like typical modern girls who have so many boyfriends. While Simran told her mother that she loved Kailash with her heart and soul and wanted to spend the rest of her life with him.

Meanwhile Kailash got offers from few law firms in Delhi. He selected two of them and went to Delhi for an interview. He went first to Ramchand & Mangaldas Law firm and had a nice chat and discussion with them. They were very satisfied with his credentials and experience and did offer him a job. Kailash however wanted to meet and see the other firm before making up his mind. He then went to meet Luthra & Luthra where he was able to negotiate more favourable terms especially that they were happy for him to manage his personal clients without any restrictions from the firm. He signed the contract for one year with Luthra & Luthra renewable at the end of the year.

Kailash informed his father about his decision who was very pleased for him. When he gave this news to his mother she was also delighted but suggested that he should first get married to Simran before he settled in Delhi. Kailash agreed and asked his parents to go ahead and make the arrangements while he looked for a suitable accommodation in Delhi and began his new job in legal practice. Kailash also wanted to find out all about corruption in legal system.

He found out that corruption is a major issue and rampant in India with adverse effects on its economy. He also found out that corrupt Indian citizens are stashing trillions of dollars in Swiss banks. One report said that Indian-owned Swiss bank account assets are worth thirteen times the national debt. Judicial corruption in India is attributable to a number of factors, including delays in the disposal of cases, shortages of judges and complex procedures, all of which are exacerbated by a preponderance of new laws. According to 'Transparency International', the judiciary in India is anti-law, anti-efficiency, anti-innocent, anti-common sense, pro-corrupt and pro-police. The judges delay the judgement so that financially strong party approaches them with money and then give judgement against the financially weak party. Kailash was disgusted with these findings but made a firm resolve to tackle the corruption sensibly.

Kailash concentrated his efforts on finding a nice house to live in Delhi. Delhi is the symbol of old India and the new, even the stones here whisper to our ears of the ages bygone and the air is full of dust and fragrances of the past, as are the fresh and piercing winds of the present. Delhi, India's capital, is the hub of the country, a buzzing international metropolis which draws people from all over India and the globe. It is a home to fifteen million people, it is big, sprawling and still growing. Yet tucked away inside Delhi's modern suburbs and developments are the tombs, temples and ruins dating back centuries. In some places, the remains of whole cities from the dim and distant past nestle among homes and highways built in just the last decade. The result is a city full of fascinating nooks and crannies that you could happily spend weeks on end exploring.

After mulling over various aspects for the location of house, Kailash concluded that south Delhi would be the ideal place for him and Simran to live in. Areas like Safdarjung, Greater Kailash, Lajpat Nagar and Janakpuri were his main choice. He managed to find a three bedroom house in Lajpat Nagar which was ready for occupation. The price was reasonable with many amenities for shopping and local transport. He discussed the purchase of the house with his father who gave him his blessings and financial support to buy that house. He had not omitted to consult Simran whom he was able take on a tour of the house on Skype. Simran appeared quite happy with the condition of the house. Simran also told him how she missed him and anxiously awaited for his tactile love. Kailash told Simran he too felt lonely without her and as soon he got possession of the house, he will visit her in Rajkot to be with her. A few weeks later Kailash duly got possession of and the keys to the house. It was in good condition but needed a woman's touch to decorate the house.

Kailash had a call from his mother telling him that all preparations were in place for his engagement to Simran. In Gujarati community the engagement ceremony is known as *Gol Dhana* literally means 'Jaggery and Coriander seeds' which are distributed to friends and family. Both their families had decided to get Kailash and Simran engaged and get them married within a week. Kailash reached Rajkot and got duly engaged to Simran in a simple exchange of ring ceremony. The preparations of their wedding the following Sunday got underway in ernest. Kailash's and Simran's parents wanted a simple wedding without any dowry because both their parents were dead against this scourge of Indian social system. All they wanted was a Vedic wedding ceremony with all the Hindu rituals which are recited in Sanskrit around sacred fire called *Agni*.

First wedding ritual is *Barat* the wedding procession which started from Kailash's house for Simran's house. It was followed by *swagatam* where Kailash and his family were welcomed by Simran's parents. Simran's mother then placed the 'red dot' on Kailash's forehead and led him to the *mandap*. Next ritual was '*Ganesh Puja*', veneration of the Hindu deity of peace and wisdom who removes any obstacles that may arise. This was followed by *Madhuparka* whereby Simran's mother washed Kailash's feet and offered him *Panchamrut* a liquid made of 5 substances i.e. milk, yogurt, ghee, honey and sugar.

Kanyadan was performed next whereby Simran's father gave away his daughter to the groom in the presence of the large gathering who were invited to witness the wedding. The *vivah* or the wedding was performed by the pandit, a Hindu priest, who tied Kailash's shoulder wear with Simran's head-cover in a nuptial knot symbolizing the sacred union and the bride and groom garlanded each other. The sacred fire, the sanctifier of the sacrament, was installed and worshiped as directed by the pandit. *Mangal phera* was done by Kailash and Simran holding their hands and going round the sacred fire three times.

The seven sacred steps were next taken by Kailash and Simran as guided by pandit chanting Vedic mantras:

1	The first step represents a vow to nourish each other
2	The second step to grow together in strength
3	The third step to preserve our wealth
4	The fourth step to preserve our joys and sorrows
5	The fifth step to care for our children
6	The sixth step to be together forever
7	The seventh step to remain lifelong friends

The pandit explained to Kailash and Simran that two perfect halves make a perfect whole and the ceremony ended with a prayer that this union was now indissoluble and he pronounced them husband and wife. Kailash also put on '*Mangal Sutra*', a chain around Simran's neck and put red vermilion on the parting of Simran's hair symbolizing her as a married woman. This was followed by blessings by the groom's and bride's parents and also by the friends and family who showered them with rose petals. All the guests were served the traditional Gujarati vegetarian meal. Simran parted from her parents with tearful eyes and accompanied Kailash to his house. They also modified the typical Gujarati tradition by inviting only the selected close friends and family and not the whole community. The intention was to save unnecessary and wasteful expenses at wedding and use the hard earned money from their parents to help with setting up their house in Delhi instead.

Savitri, Kailash's mother welcomed Simran in her house with *Aarti puja* for the new bride and let her spill an urn containing rice with her right foot in accordance with Hindu tradition. She then placed the vermillion on Simran and Kailash's foreheads with her blessings. Simran and Kailash touched Savitri and Mohan Das's feet for blessings. Their room was adorned with fresh flowers without wasting too much money on unnecessarily ostentatious decoration. They had previously decided to forgo their honeymoon because Simran was very keen to go to Delhi with Kailash and set up their home.

Kailash and Simran left for Delhi after spending two days at Rajkot. Simran was thrilled with excitement to see her house in Delhi. Kailash had taken a one month leave to be with her. They were together all the time sharing tenderness and love. She found Kailash to be a perfect husband. He was very gentle and never hurried or rushed her for anything. They would shop together and Kailash used to value her opinion. He always appreciated her cooking and sensible shopping. He was a romantic at heart as well. He had romanced to her heart and mind first before touching her body for lovemaking. He used to communicate in a sensual way that brought about erotic feelings within her. He was a passionate lover and she was grateful to God for providing her with such an understanding husband. Alas one month of honeymoon holiday at home came to an end very quickly. Time does not stand still. Kailash went back to work. His partners were pleased to see him back and congratulated him on his marriage.

Soon Kailash got busy with his work. His first client was a worker in a company who was sacked by his employer over a minor argument on pay. In fact, the employer wanted to reduce his workforce because the company was not making much profit. The worker had requested some advance payment for his daughter's wedding but the

143

cunning employer not only refused but also sacked him for it, even though the worker had been with the company for over ten years. Kailash took on this case and not only won the case but managed to get a fair compensation for unfair dismissal of the worker. A victory in his very first case was welcomed by his partners at Luthra & Luthra. Simran also congratulated Kailash on his success.

This success of this case boosted confidence in Kailash. More cases started coming his way. He wanted a wider experience of Indian law and hence he accepted all types of cases. His clients were very happy with him. Kailash charged minimal fees and in some cases he did not charge at all. His failure rate was negligible. Soon he became a popular lawyer in Delhi, but it took him three years to establish himself as a high court lawyer. His firm Luthra & Luthra also started getting more clients because of Kailash.

Kailash's parents were delighted with the progress and success of their son. His mother now wanted Kailash to plan a family. Simran was also keen to have a child as she was getting weary of sitting alone and waiting for Kailash after his long days at the office and court. Kailash understood the feelings of Simran and his parents. His father was due to retire within a year and his mother wanted to see grandchildren.

Soon Simran got pregnant and Kailash conveyed the good news to his and Simran's parents. Everybody was over the moon at the news and longingly waited for the arrival of the baby in a few month's time. Kailash's parents moved to Delhi after his father's retirement and Simran felt reassured that her mother-in-law would be there to help her look after the baby after delivery. Unfortunately Simran had a difficult labour. She was admitted to the hospital four weeks before delivery due to bleeding. It was touch and go. Kailash and his parents were very worried. But Kailash managed to keep going with his clients's concerns, secure in the knowledge that his parents were there to take care of Simran. She gave birth to a baby boy two weeks before her due date. She had to have caesarian delivery. She lost a lot of blood and needed blood transfusion. She also had a rupture of her uterus during

144

delivery and was told by the attending doctor that she should not go for a second pregnancy because it may result in complications.

Simran came home with a healthy little boy whom they named Ravi. Her mother-in-law happily took care of the baby and Simran who had become very weak and took a few weeks to recover from her difficult delivery. Kailash and his parents were very happy to have Ravi around the house who had become the cynosure of the entire family. As Kailash became busier in his law practice, Simran and his parents cheerfully looked after Ravi and watch him grow, see him sitting, crawling, standing and eventually running all around the house.

Kailash soldiered on with his crusade against corruption. He used to take only those cases where he was convinced that his clients were genuine. He would not take a case just for money even if he was offered an exorbitant amount of money. Because of his fame many rich people wanted him to take their cases offering him money underhand to persuade him. He made it a firm principle of his life and made it very clear to everybody, that he was not corruptible. In general, he took cases for the needy and middle class people who otherwise could not afford high fees charged by other expensive lawyers.

When Kailash's son Ravi was five years old, tragedy struck the Gohil family. Savitri, his mother had a lump in her breast which she was very reticent to discuss with anybody, as most elderly Indian ladies invariably are, being very shy to talk about problems with private organs of their bodies. When she started getting dizzy spells Kailash insisted that she should consult a doctor. The lady doctor, Dr Sushma found Savitri with lack of blood in her body. When the doctor examined the lump in her left breast she suspected cancer. She had a scan and a needle biopsy done which showed advanced cancer of breast with spread in the liver and lungs. It obviously affected the whole Gohil family. Kailash and his father Mohan Das discussed the prognosis with the doctor. Dr Sushma informed them that Savitri had an advanced inoperable cancer. She can have chemotherapy and radiotherapy but there are many side effects especially she will lose her hair. They asked the doctor whether it will increase her life expectancy.

145

Dr Sushma told them that it may not prolong her life much because she had only few months to live. Kailash told the doctor that they would discuss it with Savitri and would let her know their decision in few days.

Savitri was very reluctant to have chemotherapy or radiotherapy considering so many side effects. Kailash asked his mother whether there was anything or any wish she had, to make her happy in last few months of her life. Savitri said she had never been out of India and she had heard so much about Vatican in Rome and Sistine Chapel, she would like to visit these before she left the earth to meet her creator. Kailash promised that he will make arrangements so that they could visit Vatican City.

It took Kailash six weeks to arrange everything including passport, visa and tickets to visit Vatican City State. Vatican City is a landlocked sovereign city-state and is a walled enclave within the city of Rome. It was established an independent state in 1929 and has population of just eight hundred. The Pope is also the head of state and the government of the Vatican City State. The Vatican Museums are located within the city's boundaries. They display the immense art collection built up by the Roman Catholic Church through the centuries including the most important masterpieces of Renaissance art in the world. The Sistine Chapel with its ceiling decorated by Michelangelo and the Santaz della Segnatura by Raphael are the famous sites in Vatican city.

Savitri along with the whole Gohil family was awestruck to see the paintings by Michelangelo and the various sculptures. They saw the best of Gothic art in the world. Savitri enjoyed the Vatican City but was very tired and requested Kailash that since her last wish had been fulfilled, she would like to go back home in India and rest there.

Gohil family returned home and Savitri was now glad to be back in India. She now wanted to die in peace. Soon she started experiencing pain in her bones and body due to cancer spread. Doctors wanted to admit her in the hospital to make her comfortable but Savitri wanted to stay home. So she was given morphine like drugs to control her pain. The nurse used to visit their home regularly to give her comfort and medications as necessary. She survived only a few weeks after visiting Vatican City. Kailash, Mohan Das and Simran also looked after her as much as possible but could not prevent her inevitable death.

Kailash was very sad at the loss of his mother. He remembered the poem by the English poet Shelly.

> Lost angel of ruined paradise
> She knew not it was her own
> As with no stain
> She faded, like a cloud
> Which had over wept its rain

Savitri had expressed her wishes to her family that her ashes be scattered in Rameshwaram which is in the south Indian state of Tamilnadu. It is located on Pamban Island at the very tip of Indian peninsula. It is connected to mainland India by the Pamban Bridge. Rameshwaram is the terminus of the railway line between Chennai and Madurai. Together with Varanasi, it is considered to be one of the holiest places in India. According to Hindu mythology, this is the place from where the Hindu god Rama built a bridge, across the sea to Sri Lanka to rescue and liberate his wife Sita from her abductor Ravana. Kailash and Mohan Das came to Rameshwaram and duly scattered the ashes in the sea.

Kailash went straight back to work after his mother's death. It took him sometime to come to terms with the situation and get back into routine. He was again spending most of his time in the office or in court. He now made it a point to go for a daily walk early in the mornings around the banks of river Yamuna which is the largest tributary river of the Ganges. It made him relax, and he was able to think clearly about the cases and contemplate about the strategy he would adopt to deal with in the court. He also developed a habit of listening to the news on television in the evenings.

One evening he heard a shocking news on the television regarding an under construction twelve storey shopping mall which had suddenly collapsed killing several hundred workers and many seriously injured. He was very sad at this tragic news and was even more upset to know that the builder had got away scot-free in a hurriedly arranged inquest into this tragic incident. A foreman working for that builder was jailed for a mere five years.

The crash of this building shook him to his roots. The images were devastating. The clouds of dust and dirt with leaping flames of fire created an inferno where human bodies were burnt alive.

He was deeply moved. "Why does this happen? Why there is no rigorous Health and Safety at work culture in our country? Why should this go unpunished?" He ruminated.

The following day the chief minister visited the site of the mall. Standing on the rubble, that was still smoldering, with a fake expression of sorrow announced a compensation of Rs 10,000 for each worker who had died. Kailash was outraged as he knew very well that this paltry sum of money would not last for more than two months. What will happen then? The minister also declared the tragedy as an accident and closed the case. He then left the site in his shiny black Mercedes, wearing thick garlands of yellow flowers.

Kailash decided then that he would not let this go without an investigation and punishment for those who were responsible for this great human tragedy.

He visited their neighbourhood following day and was abhorred looking at the faces of woman and children who were widowed and orphaned. He knew their futures would be bleak. The union leader Prakash told him how much negligence and corruption was involved in this project. Kailash became very emotional and he swore that he will not rest until he brings justice to the victims of this tragedy.

Kailash, at the request of the union leader Prakash started investigations and he found evidence of corruption in building works of the mall. He decided to hire international private investigators Kroll Investigation Agency to find out who were involved in the chain of corruption. Kroll was founded in 1972 by Jules B Kroll to help clients improve operations by uncovering kickbacks. Kroll is headquartered in New York and has offices in many cities in the US and in London. After six weeks they reported back to Kailash, who was shocked by the report. It told all about the builder and his greed. He also came to know about the chain of corruption.

The budget sanctioned for the shopping mall project was one thousand crores rupees. However, everybody had taken their share from that budget including the minister, building inspector and the registration department. After all the cuts , the remainder money for construction became significantly reduced and the builder had to resort to using cheap cement and shoddy building materials. As a result the building collapsed. He came to know that builder had made the foreman the scapegoat. The builder had asked the foreman to take the blame in return for a guaranteed full financial support for his family until he would be released from the jail.

Kailash filed a case against the builder. In a couple of months the case came to the court.

The court was packed. It was a field day for the media. Kailash's father, now retired, was sitting next to him on the prosecuting table. He actually had advised him against getting involved in this case as during his long career in law he had seen enough corruption and conspiracies where one can lose his life trying to raise voice against the criminals. But once Kailash had decided to go forward his father became fully supportive.

The builder was present in the court and had a mock smile on his face and a touch of arrogance which showed his confidence that no harm will come his way. He had arranged the best defence team that money could buy. But Kailash was armed with the evidence provided by the Kroll Investigation Agency. He surprised them by showing evidence of transferring millions of rupees to Swiss banks by the builder. This was irrefutable evidence. He also requested the presiding judge to summon the minister in the court the following day as he had some more surprises.

The defence team was crushed when the judge indeed ordered the minister to appear in the court the following morning. Kailash also requested the judge to allow him to project a few slides that morning.

That evening his father applauded him on his success over a hot cup of tea. While being proud of his son, he was also sombre and worried. He told Kailash that this matter was getting serious and he is afraid, really afraid, where it would take him. May be a settlement might be a better choice but Kailash was seething with anger, and he politely brushed aside his father's suggestion.

In the court the next morning he requested the minister to take the witness stand. Kailash, then moved slowly but with the confident steps towards the stand. After asking a few polite questions, he looked straight into the eyes of the minister and said, "Mr Minister, sir, did you have any involvement or did you receive any gifts regarding this project?"

"Definitely not," retorted the minister contemptuously.

Kailash then asked his law clerk to turn on the projector. There was an ominous silence in the court. All eyes were on the screen. There was a transaction receipt of ten crore of rupees credited to a Swiss bank account belonging to the minister. The dates tallied with the start of the building project. Kailash, in the most dramatic way did not speak a word. The court room was engulfed in a frightening silence. Kailash let the message sink in. Then he said: " No further questions, my lord."

The lead defence advocate Mr Bijlani himself was tongue-tied.

It was obvious to all the observers and the builder that proceedings were not going their way.

The honourable judge Zakir Hussain gave forty eight hour break to both Kailash and Mr Bijlani to present their final arguments before he gave his judgment. Kailash came home in the evening and his father Mohan Das and his wife Simran were very pleased with his line of argument in defence of the poor workers. The television also was blazing with hot news about how brilliantly Kailash had presented the case against the builder. They all had a quiet family dinner. Kailash was relaxing after dinner when an anonymous phone call came with a harsh voice that warned him to withdraw the case against the builder or else he would be killed along with his family.

He told his father and Simran about this call. His father asked him to be firm but Simran was very fearful. She wanted him to withdraw from the case because she was afraid she might lose him. Kailash replied that he had embarked on this crusade against corruption and was determined to abide by the truth and fair play no matter what came in his way. Both he and Simran were very uncomfortable that night and could not sleep. In the morning, he got ready to go to his office. When he opened the door he found a parcel lying outside the house. When he opened the parcel, it contained a tin of biscuits with a note that if he did not withdraw from the case, it would be a bomb next time.

Kailash was normally a man of strong nerves, but the bomb threat shook him. He thought of his son Ravi, of his wife Simran and almost felt that he cannot go ahead with this. He, after all, had to think of himself and his family. But in this fleeting moment of weakness, an image of a face flashed in front of his eyes. As if in a trance, he saw the widow who was present in the court. Her face was ashen, her hair dishevelled and two little frightened children were tugging at her sari. With her hollow and lustreless eyes she was asking, "Will you not fulfill your promise to bring justice to me?" Kailash jerked out of his trance and found a new strength. He decided, come what may, he would not rest until he achieved what he had set out to do.

The following day after the court proceeding, he was met by a respectable looking man, who took him in a corner, smiled and told him he was his well wisher. He suggested a large sum could be transferred into his account if he dropped the case or agreed to settle. As Kailash refused, the man then said in a menacing manner that he was sorry that Kailash had not listened to his well wisher. He wished Kailash good luck and disappeared in the crowd.

Later that evening, Kailash wanted to have some peace and quiet and a bit of soul searching. Clearly, he was going to win the case. He liked the bank of the river Yamuna , especially where there was the shrine of Mahatma Gandhi.

It was a fine starry night. A gentle breeze was blowing and the trees were swaying, he was walking along the shore. The waves of the river were lapping at the sandy banks of the river. There was peace and tranquility in the atmosphere. He was pleased with himself. Suddenly, from behind a bunyan tree, a man came face to face with him, no words were exchanged. He pulled out a gun, looked into the eyes of Kailash and emptied the whole chamber. With a big thud Kailash fell on the ground, his right hand outstretched and his face turned as if he was looking at the samadhi of the great Mahatma whose ideals and teaching he was trying to follow.

He was taken by ambulance to Delhi Heart & Lung Institute and was admitted to the intensive care unit. Simran and Mohan Das rushed to the hospital when they heard the news. Doctors told them that he was in a critical state and they were doing their best to save him. He had lost a lot of blood and they were giving him blood transfusion.

Kailash was half conscious and half dreaming. The sky was a misty pumpkin shade, then a deep turquoise, then a bright lime. He was levitating. His consciousness felt smoky, wisp-like, incapable of anything but calm. He was floating over a vast yellow sea. The water changed to vapour and rose higher, became rain and came down again, became spring, brook and river with a violet colour. Kailash listened, he was listening intently, completely absorbed, quite empty, taking in everything. He felt that he had now completely learned the art of listening. His face looked peaceful and like the one who has found salvation.

Suddenly he heard a resonant voice which he had heard before but could not remember when and where. He was in a trance.

"Kailash your time on Earth has come to an end."

"Are you the Angel of Death? " Kailash asked.

"No my child, I am your Lord, The Supreme Creator," The voice countered.

"Where am I, my Lord?"

"You are in heaven my child."

"How did I deserve this?" Kailash asked.

"Because now your soul has been purified," God replied.

"Do you know all about me and my sufferings?" asked Kailash.

"Yes my child, I know everything about you and even the things before you were born. I also know the people who have affected your life," the voice replied.

"How does this work?" Kailash asked.

"Do you know the law of reincarnation?" The voice quizzed.

"Not quite," Kailash conceded.

"Reincarnation is a process of purifying the soul. You are born to serve the humankind. Everybody is made in the image of God, but by identification with the physical body, along with its imperfections and limitations," the voice replied.

"What must be done to achieve perfection?" Kailash enquired.

"Strive to do good deeds and help people and serve humanity," the voice replied.

"Do you know all about my life?" Kailash asked.

"Yes, you were Kishore in your first life and you transgressed God's laws repeatedly," the voice replied.

"And after that?" Kailash asked.

"You were named Krishin in your second life, where you had sacrificed your life for the sake of bringing peace between two estranged nations," the voice went on.

"And after that?" Kailash continued.

"Still you had not done enough to purify your soul. You were Kailash this time and you have created big waves in the sea of corruption and you have been granted salvation," the voice replied.

"Is it going to end the corruption?" Kailash asked.

"No, it is in the human blood but if everybody makes an effort, it may disappear one day," the voice responded.

At that very moment all his monitors started blinking, the ventilator became erratic and the sounds of the alarms tore the silence and sanctity of the room. Doctors and nurses ran into the room but Kailash had gone. He had a glow of eternal peace on his face. This serene glow was suffused with a colour that was beyond description like an eighth colour of the rainbow. Doctors pronounced him dead.

Stop and consider! Life is but a day
A fragile dew-drop on its perilous way
From a tree's summit; a poor Indian's sleep
While his boat hastens to the monstrous steep

Keats

The earth provides enough to every Man's needs
But not every Man's greed

Mahatma Gandhi

Acknowledgments

These stories are based on real incidents drawing heavily on my own interest in and observations of human nature over the years. It will be remiss of me if I did not acknowledge the help from:

1 Ashok Jeswani for advising me on the intricacies of Law and how the lawsuits are dealt with in the British and Indian courts.

2 Man's Eternal Quest: Sri Sri Paramhansa Yogananda for an understanding the philosophy of the reincarnation.

3 Google and Wikipedia to back up and research factual data.

4 An Autobiography: M. K. Gandhi.

5 Quotes of Gandhi: Kamal and Zahava Sharma.

6 Above all from my lifelong friend Dr. Feroz Alam who helped me in compiling the title story of the book.

7 Last but not the least Rifat Shamim for his moral support and help with writing all my books.